No one writes romantic fiction like Barbara Cartland.

Miss Cartland was originally inspired by the best of the romantic novelists she read as a girl —writers such as Elinor Glyn, Ethel M. Dell and E. M. Hull. Convinced that her own wide audience would also delight in her favorite authors, Barbara Cartland has taken their classic tales of romance and specially adapted them for today's readers.

Bantam is proud to publish these novels—personally selected and edited by Miss Cartland—under the imprint

**BARBARA CARTLAND'S
LIBRARY OF LOVE**

Bantam Books by Barbara Cartland
Ask your bookseller for the books you have missed

Barbara Cartland's Library of Love

Barbara Cartland's Library of Love
Charles Rex
by Ethel M. Dell

Condensed by Barbara Cartland

BANTAM BOOKS · TORONTO · NEW YORK · LONDON

CHARLES REX
A Bantam Book / May 1978

ISBN 0–553–11560–X

Published simultaneously in the United States and Canada

Bantam Books are published by Bantam Books, Inc. Its trade-
mark, consisting of the words "Bantam Books" and the por-
trayal of a bantam, is registered in the United States Patent
Office and in other countries. Marca Registrada. Bantam
Books, Inc., 666 Fifth Avenue, New York, New York 10019.

PRINTED IN THE UNITED STATES OF AMERICA

Introduction

I know every reader will be fascinated, as I was, by the wicked and raffish Lord Rex, and will long for him to find the true love we all seek.

Ethel M. Dell was, is and always will be, compulsive reading.

Chapter One

"I shall go to sea tomorrow," said Saltash with sudden decision. "I'm tired of this place, Larpent—fed up to repletion."

"Then by all means let us go, My Lord!" said Larpent with the faint glimmer of a smile behind his beard, which was the only expression of humour he ever permitted himself.

Saltash turned and surveyed the skyline over the yacht's rail. His eyes were odd, one black, one grey, giving a curiously unstable appearance to a countenance which otherwise might have claimed to possess some strength.

His brows were black and deeply marked. He had a trick of moving them in conjunction with his thoughts, so that his face was seldom in absolute repose.

It was said that there was a strain of royal blood in Saltash, and in the days before he had succeeded to the title, when he had been merely Charles Burchester, he had borne the nickname of "the merry Monarch."

Certain wild deeds in a youth that had not been beyond reproach had seemed to warrant this, but of later years a friend had bestowed a more gracious title upon him, and to all who could claim intimacy with him he had become "Charles Rex."

The name fitted him like a garment, and at thirty-six a certain arrogance, a certain royalty of bearing, both utterly unconscious and wholly unfeigned, characterized him.

"Yes," he said after a thoughtful silence, "we will certainly put to sea tomorrow—unless . . ."

He turned his head and threw a merry grin at his companion.

". . . unless Fortune has any tricks up her sleeve for me, I am going ashore for one more fling tonight."

"We shall be ready to start as soon as you come aboard, My Lord," Larpent replied.

"Good!" said Saltash lightly. "I may be late or—more probably—very early. Leave the gangway for me! I'll let you know when I'm aboard."

His look became suddenly speculative.

"Have you ever been in love, Larpent?"

"Once," he replied briefly.

"Only once?" gibed Saltash. "Man alive! Why, I've had the disease scores of times, and you are half a generation older than I am!"

"I know. You've had it so often that you take it lightly."

"You apparently took it like the plague," Saltash laughed.

"I didn't die of it," said Larpent grimly.

"Perhaps the lady did!" suggested Saltash.

"No. She didn't die either. For all I know she may be living now."

Saltash's grin became a grimace.

"Oh, heavens, Larpent! And you've had indigestion ever since? How long ago is it? Twenty years?"

"About that," said Larpent.

"Heavens!" said Saltash again. "I should like to see the woman who could hold me after twenty years."

"So should I," said Larpent drily.

Saltash snapped his fingers.

"She doesn't exist, my good fellow! But if she did, by Jove, what a world it would be!"

"It wouldn't be large enough to hold you, My Lord," Larpent grunted sardonically.

"Well, I'm going ashore tonight. Who knows what the gods may send? Wish me luck!"

Larpent surveyed the restless figure with a sort of stony humour.

"I wish you a safe return."

Saltash laughed and went away along the deck with a monkeylike spring that was curiously characteristic of him.

As he entered the hotel gardens a sound broke through the stillness, and in a moment he had sprung to alertness. It was a cry, a sharp wrung cry close to him, and instantly following it a flood of angry speech in a man's voice and the sound of blows.

"Damnation!" said Saltash and sprang for a narrow wooden door in the stone wall a few yards higher up.

It opened to his imperious hand, and he found himself in a dark little shrubbery behind an arbour that looked out to the sea.

It was in this arbour that the scuffle was taking

place, and in a second he had forced his way through the intervening shrubs and was at the entrance.

"Damnation!" he burst forth again furiously. "What are you doing? Leave that boy alone!"

A man in evening dress was gripping a fair-haired lad, who wore the hotel livery, by the back of his neck and raining merciless blows upon his uncovered head.

He turned sharply, straightening himself at Saltash's tempestuous entrance, and revealed to the newcomer the deeply suffused countenance of the hotel-manager.

Their recognition was mutual. He flung the boy into a corner and faced his patron, breathing hard, his black eyes still fiercely gleaming.

"Ah! It is Milord!" he said in jerky English and bowed punctiliously, though he was still shaking with rage. "What can I do for you, Milord?"

"What the devil is the matter?" said Saltash, sweeping aside all ceremony. "What are you hammering that unfortunate boy for? Can't you find a man your own size to hammer?"

The Italian flung a fierce glance over his shoulder at his crouching victim.

"He is worthless! I give him a trial—*bueno*— but he is worthless. Milord will pardon me, he is . . . English. And the English are . . . no good for work—no good at all."

"Oh, rotten to the core!" agreed Saltash with a humorous lift of the brows. "But you needn't murder him for that, Antonio. It's his misfortune —not his fault."

"Milord, I have not murdered him," the manager protested with nervous vehemence. "I have only punished him. I have not hurt him. I have done him good."

"Oh!" said Saltash and looked down at the small, trembling figure in the corner. "It's medicine, is it? But a bit strong for a child of that size. I should try a milder dose next time."

Antonio laughed harshly.

"The next time, Milord, I shall take him . . . so . . . and wring his neck!"

"Let's have a look at this specimen, with your permission," said Saltash with a smile.

He bent over the huddled figure.

"Hold up your head, boy! Let me see you!"

There was no movement to obey, and he laid a hand upon the quivering shoulder and felt it shrink away convulsively.

"I believe you've damaged him," he said, bending lower. "Here, Tommy! Hold up your head! Don't be afraid. It's a friend."

But the narrow figure only sank down a little lower under his hand.

"His name is Toby," said Antonio with acidity. "A dog's name, Milord, and it fits him well. He is what you would call a lazy hound."

Saltash paid not the slightest attention to him. He was bending low, his dark face in shadow.

"Don't be afraid!" he said again. "No one is going to hurt you. Come along! Let's look at you!"

His hold tightened upon the shrinking form. He began to lift it up.

And then suddenly there came a sharp struggle between his hands as lacking in science as the fight of a wild animal for freedom, and as effectual.

With a gasping effort the boy wrenched himself free and was gone. He went like a streak of lightning, and the two men were left facing one another.

"What a slippery little devil!"

"Yes," said Antonio vindictively. "A devil indeed, Milord! And I will have no more of him. I would have no more. I hope he will starve!"

"How awfully nice of you, Antonio!" said Saltash lightly. "Being the end of the season, he probably will."

Antonio smacked his red lips with relish.

"Ah, probably! Probably!"

*   *   *

Saltash wandered along with his face to the water, on which a myriad coloured lights rocked and swam. And still his features wore that monkeyish look of unrest, of discontent and quizzical irony oddly mingled.

He felt the lure, but it was not strong enough. Its influence had lost its potency.

He need not have been alone. He had left the hotel with friends, but he had drifted away from them in the crowd.

One of them, a girl, had sought somewhat palpably to keep him near her and he had responded with some show of ardour for a time, but then something about her had struck a note of discord within him and the glamour had faded.

"Little fool!" he murmured to himself. "She'd give me her heart to break if I'd have it."

And then he laughed in sheer ridicule of his own jaded senses. He recognized the indifference of satiety. An easy conquest no longer attracted him.

He began to stroll towards the quay, loitering here and there as if to give the Fates a chance to keep him if they would.

Yes, Sheila Melrose was a little idiot. Why couldn't she realize that she was but one of the hundreds with whom he flirted day by day?

She was nothing to him but a pastime, a toy to amuse his wayward mood. He had outgrown his earlier propensity to break his toys when he had done with them. The sight of a broken toy revolted him now.

He was impatiently aware that the girl was watching him from the middle of the shifting crowd. What did she expect? he asked himself irritably. She knew him. She knew his reputation.

Did she imagine herself the sort of woman to hold a man of his stamp for more than the passing moment? Save for his title and estates, was he worth the holding?

A group of laughing Italian girls with kerchiefs on their heads surrounded him suddenly, and he became the centre of a shower—a storm—of confetti. His mood changed in a second.

He would show her what to expect!

Without an instant's pause he turned upon his assailants, caught the one nearest to him, snatching her off her feet; and gripping her without mercy, he kissed her fiercely and shamelessly till she gasped with delicious fright, then dropped her and seized another.

The girls of Valrosa spoke of the Englishman with bated breath and shining eyes long after Saltash had gone his unheeding way, for the blood was hot in his veins before the game was over.

Wherever he went a spirit of wild daring, of fevered gaiety, surrounded him. He was no longer alone, whichever way he turned.

Once in his mad progress he met Sheila Melrose face to face, and she drew back from him in open disgust. He laughed at her maliciously, mockingly, as his royal forefather might have laughed long ago, and passed on with the throng.

Hours later, when the *fête* was over and the shore quite silent under the stars, he came alone along the quay, moving with his own peculiar arrogance of bearing, a cigarette between his lips, a deep gleam in his eyes.

It had been an amusing night after all.

Crossing the gangway to his yacht, *The Night Moth*, that rocked softly on the glimmering ripples, he paused for a moment and turned his face as if in farewell towards the little town that lay sleeping among its cypress-trees.

"Adieu, most exquisite and most wicked!" he said. "I return—no more!"

He whistled a careless air as he went below. The magic of Valrosa had loosed its hold, and he was thinking of the wide ocean and buffeting waves that awaited him.

He turned on the lights of the saloon and stopped there for another cigarette and a drink, first walking to and fro, finally flinging himself on a crimson velvet settee and surrendering himself luxuriously to a repose for which he had not felt the need until that moment.

So lying, he heard the stir and tramp of feet above him, the voices of men, the lifting of the gangway; and presently the yacht began to throb as though suddenly endowed with life.

He felt the heave of the sea as she left her moorings, and the rush of water pouring past her keel as she drew away from the quay.

He stretched himself with lazy enjoyment. It was good to come and go as he listed, good to have no ties to bind him. He supposed he would always be a wanderer on the face of the earth, and, after all, wandering suited him best.

True, there were occasions on which the thought of home allured him. The idea of marriage with some woman who loved him would spring like a beacon out of the night in moments of depression. Other men found a permanent abiding-place and were content; why not he?

But he only played with the notion. It did not seriously attract him. He was not a marrying man, and, as he had said to Larpent, the woman did not exist who could hold him.

The bare thought of Sheila Melrose sent a mocking smile to his lips. Did she think—did she really think—that she possessed the necessary qualifications to capture a man of his experience?

He dismissed her with a snap of the fingers. Sheila had practically everything in life to learn, and he did not propose to be her teacher.

All the appointments of the yacht were of the most luxurious order. She possessed every imaginable contrivance for the comfort of those who voyaged in her. Her state-cabins were a miracle of elegance and ease.

Saltash never took a valet when he went for a voyage. The steward attended to his clothes, and he waited on himself. He liked as much space as he could get both on deck and below.

He pushed open the door of his cabin and

felt for the switch of the electric light. But he did not press it when he found it, something made him change his mind.

The faint light of stars upon rippling water came to him through the open porthole and he shut himself in and stepped forward to the couch beneath it to look forth.

But as he moved, another influence caught him and he stopped short.

"Is anyone here?" he said.

Through the wash of the water he thought he heard a slight movement, and he felt a presence, as of some small animal, in the space before him.

Swiftly he stepped back, and in a moment his hand was on the switch. The light flashed on and he stood staring at a fair-haired, white-faced lad in a brown livery with brass buttons who stood staring back at him with wide, scared eyes.

Saltash was the first to recover himself; he was seldom disconcerted, never for long.

"Hullo!" he said with a quizzical twist of the eyebrows. "You, is it? And what have you come for?"

The intruder lowered his gaze abruptly, flushing to the roots of his fair hair.

"I came to . . . to ask you something."

"Then you've come some distance to do it," said Saltash lightly, "for I never turn back. Perhaps that was your idea, was it?"

"No, no!"

With a vehement shake of the head he answered.

"I didn't think you would start so soon. I thought . . . I would be able to ask you first."

"Oh, indeed!" said Saltash.

And then unexpectedly he laid a hand upon one narrow shoulder and turned the downcast face upwards.

"Ah! I thought he'd marked you, the swine! What was he drubbing you for? Tell me that!"

A great purple bruise just above one eye testified to the severity of the drubbing; the small, boyish countenance quivered sensitively under his look.

With sudden impulse two trembling hands closed tightly upon his arm.

"Well?" said Saltash.

"Oh, please, Sir . . . please, My Lord, I mean, let me stay with you! I'll earn my keep somehow, and I shan't take up much room!"

"Oh, that's the idea, is it?" said Saltash.

"Yes, yes!"

The boy's eyes implored him, blue eyes with short black lashes that imparted an oddly childish look to a face that was otherwise thin and sharp with anxiety.

"I can do anything. I don't want to live on charity. I can work. I'd love to work for you."

"You're a rum little devil, aren't you?" said Saltash.

"I'm honest, Sir! Really I'm honest! You won't be sorry if you take me. I swear you'll never be sorry!"

"What about you?" said Saltash.

He was looking down into the upraised face with a semi-quizzical compassion in his own.

"Think you'd never be sorry either?"

A sudden smile gleamed across the drawn face.

"Of course I shouldn't! You're English."

"Ah!" said Saltash with a faintly wry expression. "Not necessarily white on that account, my friend, so don't run away with that idea, I beg! I'm quite capable of giving you a worse drubbing than the good Antonio, for instance, if you qualified for it.

"I can be a terrifically wild beast upon occasion. Look here, you imp! Are you starved or what? Do you want something to eat?"

"No, Sir, no, My Lord, not really. I often don't eat. I'm used to it."

"But why the devil not?" demanded Saltash. "Didn't they feed you over there?"

"Yes, oh, yes. But I didn't want it. I was too miserable."

The blue eyes blinked rapidly under his look as if half afraid of him.

"You little ass!" said Saltash in a voice that somehow reassured. "Sit down there! Curl up if you like, and don't move till I come back!"

He indicated the sofa and quite gently but with decision freed his arm from the nervously gripping hands.

"You won't send me back?" the boy urged with quivering supplication.

"No, I won't do that," said Saltash as he went away.

He swore once or twice with considerable energy before he returned, cursing the absent Antonio in language that would have outmatched the Italian's own.

Then, having relieved his feelings, he abruptly laughed to himself and pursued his errand with businesslike briskness.

Returning he found his *protégé* in a small heap on the sofa, with his head deep in the cushion as though he sought escape from the light.

Again the feeling of harbouring some small animal in pain came to him and he frowned. The mute misery of that huddled form held a more poignant appeal than any words.

"Look here, Toby!" he said. "I've brought you something to eat, and when you've had it you'd better get a sleep. You can tell me all about it, if you want to, in the morning."

The boy had started upright at his coming. He looked at Saltash in his quick, startled way. It was almost as if he expected a kick at any moment.

Then he looked at the tray Saltash carried and suddenly his face crumpled; he hid it in his hands.

After a brief pause, with a tremendous effort the boy pulled himself together and sat up, but he did not raise his eyes to Saltash again.

He kept them fixed upon his hands, which were tightly clasped in front of him.

"I'll do . . . whatever you tell me," he said in a low voice. "No one has ever been so . . . decent to me before."

"Have one of those rolls!" said Saltash practically. "You'll talk better with something inside you."

He seated himself on the edge of his bunk and lit another cigarette, his attitude one of royal indifference but his odd eyes flashing to and fro with a monkeylike shrewdness that missed nothing of his desolate companion's forlorn state.

"You've been doing this starvation business for some time, haven't you?" he asked presently. "No wonder you didn't feel like work."

The boy's pinched face smiled, a small wistful smile.

"I can work. I can do anything, women's work as well as men's. I can cook and clean boots and knives, and sew on buttons and iron trousers, and wash shirts and wait at table, and make beds and sweep and . . ."

"For heaven's sake, stop!" Saltash interrupted. "You make me giddy. Tell me the things you can't do instead! It would take less time."

Toby considered for a few moments.

"I can't drive cars. But I can clean 'em, and I'd love to learn."

"That's the sole exception, is it?" Saltash laughed. "You seem to have picked up a good deal in a short time. Did they teach you all that over there?"

Toby shook his head.

"I've knocked about a good lot."

"And know everything, evidently," said Saltash. "What made you think of coming on board this yacht?"

The boy's eyes gave him a shining look.

"Because she belongs to you."

"Oh!" Saltash puffed at his cigarette for a few seconds. "You'd made up your mind to throw in your fortunes with mine, had you?"

Toby nodded.

"I wanted to . . . if you'd have me."

"Seems I haven't much choice," remarked Saltash. "And what are you going to do when you're tired of me? Fling yourself at someone else's head, I suppose?"

Again he saw the hot colour flood the thin face, but the boyish eyes did not flinch from his.

"No, I shan't do that. I'll just go right under next time."

"Oh, will you?" said Saltash. "And so remain a blot on my escutcheon for all time. Well, now, look here! You say you're honest?"

"Yes, Sir," said Toby with breathless assurance and sprang up and stood before him with the words, as though challenging criticism.

Saltash poked at him with his foot as he said:

"Make me a promise?"

"Anything you wish, My Lord," said Toby promptly.

"Be careful!" Saltash grinned at him. "I see you are of a rash and impulsive disposition, and I like my slaves to have a little discretion. The promise I want is that whatever happens to you, however much I kick you or bash you or generally ill-use you, you'll never jump overboard or do anything silly of that kind. Is it done?"

Toby was standing before him, facing him with straight, candid eyes. He did not seem surprised at the suggestion so coolly made. Saltash noted that it certainly did not shock him.

"All right, Sir," he said after a moment.

"It's a promise, is it?" said Saltash.

"Yes, Sir." Toby nodded.

"Good!" said Saltash. "Did anyone see you come aboard?"

"No, My Lord."

"Then you came with me, see? I brought you, if anyone wants to know."

"Very good, My Lord. Thank you, My Lord."

Saltash made a humorous grimace.

"You can call me 'Sir' if you like. It makes no difference."

"Thank you, Sir," said Toby with a responsive grin.

"And your name is Toby, is it? Toby what?"

"Toby Wright, Sir," he replied promptly.

Saltash's eyes scrutinized him with half-derisive amusement.

"I hope it's a good fit. Well, look here, Toby, you must go to bed. Did you bring any luggage on board?"

"No, Sir. 'Fraid not, Sir. Very sorry, Sir. I came away in a hurry," explained Toby rather nervously.

"And stole the hotel livery," said Saltash.

"No, Sir. Borrowed it," said Toby.

"Ho! You're going to pay for it, are you?" questioned Saltash.

"Yes, Sir, some day. First money I get, Sir. Don't want to have anything belonging to that damn Italian cur," said Toby with much emphasis.

"Naughty! Naughty!" said Saltash, pinching his arm. "Well, come along and I'll show you where you can sleep. There's a small cabin out of my dressing-room you can have for the present. I haven't got my valet on board."

"Very good, Sir, thank you. What time shall I call you, Sir?" said Toby brightly.

"You needn't call me," said Saltash. "You can just lie quiet and take care of that black eye of yours. I'll let you know when I want you."

"Very good, Sir," said Toby, looking crestfallen.

"And you'll do as you're told, see?—always! That's understood, is it?"

Toby smiled again, eagerly, gratefully.

"Yes, Sir. Always, Sir! Shall I take off your boots before I go, Sir?"

"No. Look after yourself for the present!" said Saltash. "And don't get up to mischief! There's a very strict captain in command of this boat, so you'd better mind how you go."

The boy looked up at him with eyes of twinkling comprehension. He had plainly forgotten the despair that had so nearly overwhelmed him.

"Oh, I'll be very good, Sir," he promised. "I won't get you into trouble anyhow, Sir."

"You imp!" said Saltash, pulling his ear. "Think I'll put up with your impudence, do you? You'll play that game once too often if you're not careful."

Toby hastened to adjust his features to a becoming expression of gravity.

"I won't, Sir. No, I won't. I'll be a good servant to you, the best you've ever had. I'll never forget your goodness to me, and I'll pay back somehow, that I will, Sir."

His boyish voice suddenly throbbed with emotion and he stopped. Again for a moment he had the forlorn look of a small animal astray from its own.

Saltash patted his shoulder kindly.

"All right. That'll do. Don't be tragic about it! Come along to your burrow and have a good square sleep!"

He led him away without further words, and Toby went gratefully and submissively.

A few minutes later Saltash came back with a smile on his face, half quizzical and half compassionate.

"Rum little devil!" he commented again as he began to undress. "So the gods had a gift for me after all! Wonder what I shall do with it!"

And then abruptly the smile became a mocking grimace that banished all the kindliness from his face. He snapped his fingers and laughed.

"I wonder!" he said again.

Chapter Two

It was contrary to Captain Larpent's habit to show surprise at any time, whatever the caprices of his patron, but he did look at Saltash somewhat harder than usual when the latter informed him in his breezy fashion of the unexpected addition to the yacht's company.

"You won't want to be bothered with him," he said after brief reflection. "Better let him sleep in the fore-castle."

"Not for the present," said Saltash. "I am going to train him, and I'll keep him under my own eye. The little beggar has had a pretty rough time of it, to judge by appearances. I've a fancy for looking after him myself."

"What are you going to make of him?" asked Larpent.

Saltash laughed carelessly, flicking the ash from his cigarette.

"I'll tell you that when I can show you the finished article. I'm keeping him below for the present. He's got a prize-fighter's eye which is not exactly an ornament. Like to have a look at him? You're ship's doctor."

"P'raps I'd better. I'm not over-keen on sudden importations. You never know what they may bring aboard with them."

Saltash's eyes gleamed mischievously.

"Better inoculate the whole crew at once! He's more like a stray spaniel than anything else."

"A King Charles!" suggested Larpent with the flicker of an eyelid. "Well, My Lord, let's have a look at your latest find!"

"Here he is, Larpent! What do you think of him? A poor sort of specimen, eh?"

"What's his name?" said Larpent.

"Toby Barnes, Sir," supplied the boy promptly.

Larpent bent and looked closely at the injured eye.

"You will have to stay in bed for a week," he said after a brief examination. "And then I'll look at you again!"

"Oh, not a week!" exclaimed Toby aghast, and then clapped his hand to his mouth and was silent.

But his look implored Saltash, who laughed and pinched the shoulder under his hand.

"All right. We'll see how you get on. If we meet any weather you'll probably be only too thankful to stay there."

Toby smiled somewhat woefully and said nothing.

Larpent stood up.

."I'll fetch some stuff to dress it with. Better have it bandaged. Pretty painful, isn't it?"

"No, Sir," lied Toby valiantly. "Don't feel it at all."

But he shrank with a quick gasp of pain when Larpent unexpectedly touched the injury.

"Don't hurt the child!" said Saltash sharply.

Larpent smiled his faint, sardonic smile and turned away.

Toby laid his cheek with a winning, boyish gesture against the hand that held him.

"Don't make me go to bed, Sir! I'll be miserable in bed."

Saltash looked down at him with eyebrows comically working.

"It is rather a hole, that cabin of yours. You can lie on the couch in my state-room if you like. Don't get up to mischief, that's all! I'm responsible for you, remember."

Toby thanked him humbly, swearing obedience and good behaviour. The couch in Saltash's cabin was immediately under a porthole, and the fresh sea air blew straight in. He stretched his meagre person upon it with a sigh of contentment, and Saltash smiled down upon him.

"That's right. You'll do there. Let's see! What did you say your name was?"

"Toby, Sir."

"Toby Barnes or Toby Wright?" Saltash inquired.

The boy started, turned very red, then very white, opened his mouth to speak, shut it tightly, and said nothing.

Saltash took out his cigarette-case and opened it with great leisureliness. The smile still played about his features as he chose a cigarette. Finally he snapped the lid and looked down again at his *protégé*.

"Or Toby nothing?" he said.

Toby's eyes came up to his, though the effort to raise them drew his face painfully.

"Whatever you like, My Lord," he said faintly. "I'll answer to anything."

Saltash's own face was curiously softened. He looked down at Toby for some seconds in silence, idly tapping the cigarette he held against the case.

"How old are you?" he asked suddenly.

"Sixteen, Sir." Toby's eyes with their dumb pleading were still anxiously raised to his.

Saltash bent abruptly and put his hand very lightly over them.

"All right. Don't hurt yourself. You're young enough to chuck the past and start again."

Toby's clawlike hands came up and closed upon his wrist.

"Wish I could, Sir," he whispered with lips that quivered. "Haven't had much of a chance . . . so far, Sir."

"All right," Saltash said again. "It's up to you. I shan't interfere. Don't expect too much of me; that's all I ask. I'm not considered exactly a suitable companion for young things like you."

He drew his hand away and lighted his cigarette. Toby turned his face into the cushion and lay very still.

Some hours later, when the blow that Larpent had prophesied earlier had arrived in earnest and the yacht was pitching on a wild sea in the light of a lurid sunset, Saltash came below to change.

He was met by Toby, ghastly of face but still desperately smiling, who sprang from his couch to wait upon him and collapsed at his feet.

"Little ass!" said Saltash, barely preventing himself from tumbling headlong over him.

He lifted the slight, trembling figure and put it down upon the couch. Then he poured out a dose of brandy and water and, holding the boy's head on his arm while the yacht lifted and tossed, compelled him to drink it.

"Now you lie quiet!" he commanded. "Don't stir an eyelid till I give you leave!"

The porthole was shut and the atmosphere close and stuffy. Toby put forth an appealing hand and clung to his protector's sleeve.

"Mayn't I come on deck, Sir?" he murmured anxiously. "Please, Sir!"

"No," said Saltash.

Toby said no more, but his fingers fastened like a bird's claw on the man's arm, and he shivered.

"You're frightened!" said Saltash.

"No, Sir! No, Sir!" he protested.

"Yes, you are. You needn't bother to lie to me. I always know." Saltash's voice held an odd note of comradeship. "Beastly sensation, isn't it! Have some more brandy!"

Then, as Toby refused, he sat down abruptly on the edge of the couch and thrust an arm out to him. Toby crept to him then like a nervous dog and trembled against his side.

"Little ass!" said Saltash again. "Been lying here sweating with terror, have you? There's nothing whatever to sweat about. She's as safe as houses."

"Yes, Sir. I know, Sir," whispered Toby apologetically.

Saltash's arm surrounded him with a comforting closeness.

"You miserable little shrimp! How's the head?"

"Better, Sir. Thank you, Sir," muttered Toby.

"Why not tell the truth for once and say it hurts like hell?" suggested Saltash.

Toby was silent.

"Do you know what I'm going to do with you?" said Saltash.

"No, Sir." Toby stirred uneasily.

The vessel pitched to a sudden slant and Saltash braced himself, protecting the fair head from the blow against the woodwork behind them.

"I'm going to put you to bed in my bunk here. You've got to have a decent night's rest. Did Murray look you out any spare slops? I told him to."

"Oh, yes, Sir. Thank you, Sir. But I couldn't sleep in your bunk, Sir . . . please, Sir . . . indeed, Sir!"

Toby, still held by the sheltering arm, waxed incoherent, almost tearful.

Saltash pulled him up short.

"You'll do as I tell you, now and always. You've put yourself in my hands, and you'll have to put up with the consequences. Got that?"

"Yes, Sir," Toby replied meekly.

"Then don't forget it!" said Saltash.

Toby subsided without further protest. Perhaps the brandy helped to make him quiescent, or perhaps it was only the realization of his utter weakness and dependence; but from that moment he was as submissive as if he had been indeed the small captive animal to which his new owner had likened him.

At Saltash's behest, and with his help, he presently crept back to his own cabin to divest himself of his hotel livery and don the very roomy suit of pyjamas that Murray, the steward, had served out to him.

Then barefooted, stumbling, and shivering, he returned to where Saltash leaned smoking in the narrow dressing-room, awaiting him.

Saltash's dark face wore a certain look of grimness. He bent without words and lifted the shrinking figure in his arms.

Ten seconds later Toby sank down in a berth as luxurious as any ever carried by private yacht.

He was still shivering though a grateful warmth came about him as Saltash tucked him in. He tried to murmur thanks but ended with a quivering chin and silence.

"Go to sleep, you little ass!" commanded Saltash.

And so at last Toby slept, the deep, unstirring sleep of exhaustion, utterly unconscious of his surroundings, unaware of the man who came in and out, watching that unchanging repose, sublimely oblivious to all observation, sunk in a slumber so remote that it might have been the last long rest of all.

Saltash spent the night on the velvet couch under the closed porthole, dozing occasionally and always awaking with a jerk as the roll of the vessel threatened to pitch him on to the floor of the cabin.

It was not a comfortable means of resting, but he endured it in commendable silence with now and then a grimace which said more than words.

And the little waif that the gods had flung to him slept in his bunk all through the long hours as peacefully as an effigy upon a tomb.

*   *   *

The storm spent itself before they reached Gibraltar, and Toby emerged smiling from his captivity below.

He still wore the brown and gold hotel livery as there was nothing else on board to fit him, but from Gibraltar a small packet of notes was despatched to Antonio by Saltash in settlement of the loan.

"Now I've bought you, body and soul," he said to Toby, whose shining look showed nought but satisfaction at the announcement.

It was an odd companionship which only the isolated life they led during those few days could have developed along those particular lines.

When Saltash was bored he amused himself with his *protégé*, teaching him picquet and chess, and finding in him an apt and eager pupil. There was a good deal of the gambler's spirit in Toby, and Saltash idly fostered it because it gave him sport.

He laughed at his opponent's keenness, supplied stakes for the game, even good-naturedly let himself be beaten.

And then one day he detected Toby cheating. It was an end that he might have foreseen. He had encouraged the fever, he had practically sown the seeds; but, strangely, he was amazed, more disconcerted than he had been for years by the consequences.

For it was not his way to disturb himself over anything. His principles were easy to laxness.

But that Toby, the urchin he had sheltered and nursed like a sick puppy, should have done this thing somehow cut clean through his complacence.

"I'm going to give you a licking for that," he said, black brows drawn to a stern line. "You can go below and wait for it."

Toby went like an arrow, and Saltash spent

the next half hour pacing the deck, cursing himself, the youngster, and the insane and ridiculous Fate that had linked them together.

Then he went below to administer judicial corporal punishment to a human being for the first time in his life. As he himself whimsically expressed it, he had received ample correction during his own chequered career, but he had never been in a position to correct anyone else.

He found Toby waiting for him in his shirt-sleeves, rather white but quite composed, his riding switch all ready to his hand.

"Ever been flogged before?" he asked him curtly as he picked it up.

"No, Sir," said Toby with downcast eyes.

"Why not?" There was a gibing note in Saltash's voice. "Never qualified before?"

Toby shot him a swift and nervous glance that was like a flash of blue flame.

"No, Sir. Never been caught before."

Saltash's eyes flickered humour, but he steeled himself.

"Well, you're caught this time—fairly caught. I may not be a specially fit person to punish you for it, but you won't be let off on that account."

"Go ahead, Sir!" said Toby with his hands twisted into a bony knot in front of him.

And Saltash went ahead. His heart was not in the business, and as he smote the narrow bent back it cried shame on him.

Toby made no sound, but at the third stroke he winced, and immediately Saltash with a terrific oath in French hurled his switch violently at the opposite wall.

"There! Don't do it again!" he said and swung him round to face him.

Then he saw that Toby was crying and abruptly let him go, striding out through the dining-saloon and up the companion-way, swearing strange oaths in varied languages as he went.

*   *   *

They sighted the English shore a few days later, on an evening of mist and rain. The sea was grey and dim, the atmosphere cold and inhospitable.

"Just like England!" said Saltash. "She never gushes over her prodigals."

He was dining alone in the saloon, with Toby behind his chair, Larpent being absent on the bridge.

"Don't you like England, Sir?" Toby asked.

"I adore her," said Saltash with his most hideous grimace. "But I don't go to her for amusement."

Toby came forward to fill his glass with liqueur.

"Too strait-laced, Sir?"

Saltash nodded with a sidelong glance at the young face bent over the decanter.

"Too limited in many ways, my Toby. But at the same time useful in certain emergencies. A stern mother, perhaps, but a wise one on the whole. You, for instance—she will be the making of you."

A slight tremor went through Toby. He set down the decanter and stepped back.

"Of me, Sir?"

Saltash nodded again. He was fingering the stem of his glass, his queer eyes dancing a little.

"We've got to make a respectable citizen of you—somehow."

"Do you think that matters, Sir?" Toby enquired.

Saltash raised his glass.

"You won't always be a boy of sixteen, you know, Toby. We've got to think of the future, whether we want to or not."

"I don't see why, Sir," Toby answered.

"You see, you're young," said Saltash and drank with the air of one who drinks a toast.

Suddenly he turned in his chair, the glass still in his hand.

"Our last night on board!" he said with a royal gesture of invitation. "You shall drink with me."

Toby's face flushed burningly. He hung back.

"Not ... not from your glass, Sir! Not ... liqueur!"

"Why not? Afraid?" mocked Saltash.

Toby was silent. His hand closed involuntarily upon the back of his master's chair. The flush died out of his face.

Saltash sat and looked at him for a few seconds, still with that dancing gleam in his eyes. Then abruptly he moved, rose with one knee upon the chair, lifted the glass to Toby's lips.

"Afraid?" he said again, speaking softly as one speaks to a frightened child.

Toby raised a hand that sought to take the glass but closed instead nervously upon Saltash's wrist. He drank in response to Saltash's unspoken insistence, looking straight at him all the time.

Then oddly he smiled.

"No, not afraid, Sir. Only lest I might not bring you luck."

"Oh, don't fret yourself on that account!" said Saltash. "I'm not used to any luck."

Toby's eyes widened.

"I thought you had everything, Sir."

Saltash laughed and set down the empty glass.

"*Au contraire, mon cher*. I am no richer than you are. Like Tantalus, I can never quench my thirst. Like many a better man than I, I see the stars, but I never reach them."

"Does anybody?" said Toby in the tone of one not expecting an answer.

Saltash laughed briefly.

"I believe some people soar. But they generally come down hard in the end. Whereas those who always crawl on the earth haven't far to fall. Now look here, Toby, you and I have got to have a talk."

"Yes, Sir," said Toby, blinking rather rapidly.

Saltash was watching him with a faint smile in his eyes, half derisive and half tender.

"What are you going to be, Toby! It all turns on that."

Toby's hand still gripped the back of his chair. He stood up very straight, facing him.

"That is for you to decide, Sir."

"Is it?" said Saltash, and again his eyes gleamed a little. "Is it for me to decide?"

"Yes, Sir. For you alone."

There was no flinching in Toby's look now. His eyes were wide and very steady.

Saltash's mouth twitched as if he repressed some passing emotion.

"You mean . . . just that?" he asked after a moment.

"Just that, Sir," said Toby with a slight quickening of the breath. "I mean, I am . . . at your disposal alone."

Saltash took him suddenly by the shoulder and looked at him closely.

"Toby! Aren't you making rather a fool of yourself?"

"No, Sir!" Swiftly, with unexpected vehemence, Toby answered. "I'm doing the only thing possible. But if you . . . if you . . . if you . . ."

"Well?" Saltash said. "If I what?"

"If you want to get rid of me . . . at any time," Toby said, commanding himself with fierce effort, "I'll go, Sir. I'll go!"

"And where to?" Saltash's eyes were no longer derisive; they held something that very few had ever seen there.

Toby made a quick gesture of the hands and dropped them flat at his sides.

"I'll get rid of myself then, Sir. That won't be very difficult. And I'll do it so that you won't even know."

Saltash stood up abruptly.

"Toby, you are quite unique! Superb too in your funny little way. Your only excuse is that you're young. Does it never occur to you that you've attached yourself to the wrong person?"

"No, Sir," breathed Toby.

"You're not afraid to make all you've got on a bad card?" pursued Saltash, still curiously watching him.

"No, Sir," he said again, and added with his faint, unboyish smile, "I haven't much to lose anyway."

Saltash's hand tightened upon him. He was

smiling also, but the gleam in his eyes had turned to leaping, fitful flame.

"Well, I have never yet refused a gift from the gods."

And there he stopped, for suddenly, drowning all speech, there arose a din that seemed to set the whole world rocking, and in a moment there came a frightful shock that pitched them both headlong to the floor.

Saltash fell as a monkey falls, catching at one thing after another to save himself, landing eventually on his knees in pitch darkness, with one hand still gripped upon Toby's thin young arm.

But Toby had struck his head against a locker and had gone down stunned and helpless.

The din of a siren above them still filled the world with hideous clamour as Saltash recovered himself.

"Damn them!" he ejaculated savagely. "Do they want to deafen us as well as send us to perdition?"

Then very suddenly it stopped, leaving a void that was instantly filled with lesser sounds. There arose a confusion of voices, of running feet, a hubbub of escaping steam, and a great rush of water.

Saltash dragged himself up in the darkness, sought to drag Toby also, found him a dead weight, stooped and lifted him with wiry strength. He trod among broken glass and plates as he straightened himself.

The noise above them was increasing. He flung the limp form over his shoulder and began desperately to claw his way up a steep slant towards the saloon door and the companion-way.

Sound and instinct guided him, for the darkness was complete. But he was not the man to die like a trapped animal while the most slender way of escape remained.

Hampered as he was, he made for the open with set teeth and terrible foreign oaths of which he was utterly unconscious.

"Saltash!" cried a voice, piercing the outer din. "Saltash!"

"Here!" yelled back Saltash, still fighting for foothold and finding it against the leg of the table. "That you, Larpent? How long have we got?"

"Seconds only!" said Larpent briefly. "Give me the child!"

"No! Just give me a hand, that's all! Hang on tight! It'll be a pull."

Saltash flung himself forward again, his free hand outstretched, slipped and nearly fell on his face, then was caught by a vicelike grip that drew him upwards with grim strength.

In a moment he was braced against the frame of the door, almost standing on it, the saloon gaping below him, a black pit of destruction.

Larpent's torch showed the companion-stairs practically perpendicular above them.

"Go on!" said Larpent. "Better give me the child. It's you that matters."

"Get out, damn you!" said Saltash, and actually grinned as he began to climb with his burden still hanging upon his shoulder.

Larpent came behind him, holding his torch to light the way. They climbed up into a pandemonium indescribable, a wild torrent of sound.

A lifebuoy hanging beside the hatch caught

his eye as he glanced swiftly around, and in a second he pounced upon it. Toby slipped from his shoulder as he bent, and, slipping, awoke.

But he only lay and stared with dazed eyes at the man frantically unlashing the rope, as one who looked on from afar.

Then Larpent was with them again. He dragged Toby to his feet, and in a flash Saltash turned, the lifebuoy on his arm.

"What the devil are you doing?"

"They've got the boat free." Larpent pointed. "Go while you can!"

But Saltash barely glanced across. He put the lifebuoy over Toby's head and shoulders and began to wind the rope around him. It did not need a glance to know that the boat would never get away.

At his action Toby gasped, and sudden understanding awoke in his eyes. He dragged one arm free and made as if he would cling to Saltash.

"Keep me with you, Sir!" he cried out wildly. "Don't make me go alone!"

Saltash gripped the clutching hand, dropping the end of rope. It trailed down and Larpent caught it, flung it round Saltash's body and knotted it while he was lifting Toby over the rail.

Then for a second Saltash hung, one hand still gripping Toby's, the other holding to the rail of his sinking yacht, the two of them poised side by side above the abyss.

"You'll save yourself, Larpent!" he cried. "I shall want you."

And with that he turned suddenly to his shivering companion and actually smiled into the terrified eyes.

"Come on, Toby! We go—together!"

He flung his leg over with the words, and leapt straight downwards.

Toby's shriek sounded through the tumult as they went into the grey depths.

* * *

The sinking of *The Night Moth* after being in collision with the liner *Corfe Castle,* bound for Brazil, was an event of sufficient importance to be given a leading place in the newspapers of the following day.

Lord Saltash was well known as a private yachtsman, and the first account which reported him amongst the drowned was received with widespread regret throughout that circle in which he was a familiar figure.

Then at a later hour came the contradiction, and his friends smiled and remarked that he had the facility of an eel for getting out of tight corners, and that they would never believe him dead till they had been to his funeral.

Long before the publication of the second report Saltash was seated in the captain's cabin on board the *Corfe Castle,* with a strong brandy and soda before him, giving a brief and vigorous account of himself and his company.

"Well, I hope you don't blame us for your bad luck," the captain said. "We might have been sunk ourselves."

"I never blame anyone but the devil for that," said Saltash generously. "And as you managed to pick us all up, I am glad on the whole that you weren't."

And then he turned sharply at a knock on the

door behind him to see a lean, lank man enter who peered at him curiously through screwed-up eyes as though he had never seen anything like him before.

Captain Beaumont introduced him.

"This is Dr. Hurst. He has come to report. Well, Doctor? I hope you bring good news."

Dr. Hurst came forward to the table, still looking very attentively at Saltash.

The latter's odd eyes challenged him with royal self-assurance.

"Well? What is the news? Fished for a sprat and caught a whale, or is it t'other way round?"

The doctor cleared his throat and turned to the captain.

"Yes, my report is good on the whole. None of the men is seriously injured, thanks to your prompt rescue measures. Captain Larpent is still unconscious; he is suffering from concussion. But I believe he will recover. And . . . and . . ."

He hesitated, looking again at Saltash.

"The person whose life you saved . . ."

Saltash leaned back in his chair, grinning mischievously.

"To be sure! The person whose life I saved? What of that person, Dr. Hurst?"

"Had you a passenger?" interrupted the captain. "I understood you saved a cabin-boy."

Saltash was openly laughing in the doctor's face.

"Pray continue! What of the cabin-boy? None the worse, I hope?"

The doctor's lank figure drew together with a stiff movement of distaste.

"I see that you are aware of a certain fact

which I must admit has given me a somewhat unpleasant surprise."

Saltash turned abruptly to the captain.

"You ask me if I had a passenger. Before you also begin to be unpleasantly surprised, let me explain that I had a child on board who did not belong to the ship's company."

"A child?" Captain Beaumont looked at him in astonishment. "I thought . . . I understood . . . Do you mean the boy?"

"Not a boy, no—a girl!"

Saltash's voice was suddenly very suave; he was smiling still, but there was something rather formidable about his smile.

"A young girl, Captain Beaumont, but amply protected, I assure you. It was our last night on board. She was masquerading in the state-cabin in a page's livery when you struck us. But for Larpent we should have been trapped there like rats when the yacht went down.

"He came and hauled us out, and we saved the child between us."

He turned again to the doctor, his teeth gleaming foxlike between his smiling lips.

"Really, I am sorry to disappoint you. But the truth is seldom as highly coloured as our unpleasant imaginings. The child is . . . Larpent's daughter."

He rose with the words, still suavely smiling.

"And now, if she is well enough, I am going to ask you to take me to her. It will be better for her to hear about her father from me than from a stranger."

Though courteously uttered, his words contained a distinct command. The doctor looked at him with the hostility born of discomfiture, but he raised no protest. Somehow Saltash was invincible at that moment.

"Certainly you can see her if you wish. In fact, she has been asking for you."

"Ah!" said Saltash and relaxed into his sudden grin. "I should have thought you would be glad to get rid of me before my bad luck spreads any further."

Saltash, carelessly sauntering in the doctor's wake, found himself the object of considerable interest on the part of those passengers who were already up in the murk of the early morning.

He was stopped by several to receive congratulations upon his escape, but he refused to be detained for long. He had business below, he said, and the doctor was waiting.

And so at last he came to a cabin at the end of a long passage, at the door of which a kind-faced stewardess met them and exchanged a few works with his guide.

"Can I go in?" said Saltash, growing impatient.

The woman looked at him with wonder and compassion in her eyes.

"The poor little thing is very upset. She lies and trembles and has hardly spoken at all except to ask for you."

"Well, let me in!" said Saltash, suddenly imperious. "I've got something to tell her."

He had his way, for there was something about him that compelled just then. He entered the cabin as a king might enter the apartment of a slave, and he shut the door with decision upon those outside.

Then for a second, just for a second, he hesitated.

"Toby!"

A meagre form sprang upright in the bunk at the sound of his voice. Two bare, skinny arms reached out to him.

Then with a single stride Saltash was beside the bunk and was holding tightly to him a small, whimpering creature that hid its face very deeply against his breast and clutched at him piteously whenever he sought to raise it.

Saltash bent his dark head over the fair one and spoke very gently, yet with authority.

"It's all right, child. I know. I've known all along! Don't fret yourself! There's no need. I've got you under my protection. You're safe."

"You . . . knew!" whispered the muffled voice. "What must you . . . think?"

"I!" Saltash laughed a little. "I never think. I give everyone—always—the benefit of the doubt, which is considerably more than anyone ever gives me."

"And . . . you saved my life!" gasped Toby. "Why did you? Why did you?"

"I wanted it," said Saltash promptly. "Now listen a moment! We've done with this show. It's played out. We'll ring up on another. You've got to change your name again. I'm telling everyone you're Larpent's daughter."

That brought the fair head upwards very swiftly. The blue eyes, with their short black lashes, looked straight up to his.

"But . . . but . . . Captain Larpent . . ."

"Oh, never mind Larpent! I'll square him."

Saltash's look flashed over the pale, tear-stained face. His hold, though close, no longer compelled.

"Leave it all to me! Don't you fret! I'll square Larpent. I'll square everybody. You lie low till they put us ashore! After that, do you think you can trust me?"

He spoke with comically twisted eyebrows and a smile half kindly and half quizzical. And the forlorn little creature in his arms turned with a swooping, passionate movement, caught one of his hands and pressed it to quivering lips.

"I'll live . . . or die . . . for your sake!" the trembling voice told him. "I'm just . . . yours."

Saltash stooped abruptly and laid his face for a moment against the shorn, golden head. Just for that moment a hint of emotion showed in his strange eyes, but it was gone instantly.

He raised himself again with a grimace of self-ridicule.

"Well, look here! Don't forget to play the game! Larpent, your daddy, is knocked out, remember. He is unconscious for the present, but the doctor chap seems to think he'll be all right. A nasty, suspicious person, that doctor, so watch out! And let me see! What is Toby short for? I'd better know."

"Antoinette," whispered the lips that still caressed his hand.

"Antoinette!"

Saltash's hand closed softly upon the pointed chin, softly lifted it.

"I think *Mignonette* would suit you better," he said in his quick, caressing way. "It's time I chose a name for you, *ma chère*. I shall call you that."

"Or just Nonette of Nowhere," breathed the red lips, piteously smiling. "That would suit me best of all."

"No, no!" said Saltash and gently relinquished his hold. "Don't forget that you are a favourite of the gods! That counts for something, my Toby. They don't take up with everybody."

"They haven't done much for me so far," said Toby rebelliously.

"Hush!" said Saltash with semi-comic warning. "You are too young to say that."

"I am . . . older than you think, Sir," said Toby, colouring painfully and turning from his look.

"No, you're not! I know how old you are, child. It is written in your eyes. They have always told me all I need to know."

Then, very tenderly, as Toby's hands covered them from his look:

"Mais, Mignonette, they have never told me anything that you could wish me not to know."

He slipped his arm again about the slender shoulders and pressed them closely for a moment. Then he stood up and turned to go.

He was smiling as he went out, the smile of the gambler who knows that he holds a winning card.

Chapter
Three

It was a week after the sinking of *The Night Moth* that Saltash, very immaculately dressed, with field-glasses slung over his shoulder, made his first appearance since the disaster at a meeting on the Graydown Racecourse, a few miles from his ancient Castle of Burchester.

He was looking very well pleased with himself, and certainly none the worse for the adventure, as he sauntered among his friends, of whom a good many were present.

There had been a time, years before, when he had kept his own stud and racing had been his hobby. It had not held him for long. He was not the man to pursue any one object for any length of time.

With characteristic volatility he had thrown up this amusement to follow others, but he had never wholly abandoned his interest in the stud which had once been his.

It was now owned by one Jake Bolton, a man of rugged exterior, whose integrity had become a proverb on the Turf. This man was Saltash's erst-while trainer, and a very curious bond existed between them.

It was a showery spring day and the turf of the racecourse shone with a fresh greenness. Saltash strolled through the paddock to find Jake Bolton, whistling a careless air as he went.

"Glad you're safe and sound, My Lord," Jake said when he finally found him.

"That's uncommonly kind of you, Jake." Saltash laughed with his royal air of graciousness. "I share the sentiment. I know you would all have been heartbroken if I hadn't turned up again. How is Maud?"

"Very well, if she doesn't work too hard. I have to keep her in order in that respect," Jake Bolton answered.

"You always were a bully, but I'll bet she gets her own way all the same. So you've got a boy at last. Hope it's a good one!"

"He'd better be, hadn't he, Jake?" struck in Bunny, Maud's brother. "The imp is six months old now and goes for a canter on The Hundredth Chance every day when I'm at home. You actually haven't seen him yet, Charlie? What a rotter you were to be away all the winter!"

"Well, I'm home now anyway," said Saltash with a comical glance at Jake. "Am I to be allowed to call and view the latest acquisition?"

Jake was looking straight at him.

"Are you alone at the Castle, My Lord?"

"Of course I'm alone! What did you expect?" Saltash began to laugh. "Ah, I see!"

His glance flashed to Bunny.

"Yes, I am quite alone, most conspicuously

and virtuously unaccompanied. Come and see for yourself! Search the Castle from turret-chamber to dungeon! You will find nothing but the most monastic emptiness. I've turned into a hermit. Haven't they made that discovery yet?

"My recent deliverance from what I must admit was a decidedly awkward predicament in the Channel has sobered me to such an extent that on my life I begin to doubt if I shall ever be anything but a dull dog again."

Jake grinned.

"Yes, that's the truth, Jake. You can take it or leave it. But I'm coming to see Maud in any case. When is my presence least likely to cause you inconvenience?"

"Oh, damn it, Jake!" broke in Bunny with sudden heart. "You know Maud said you were to ask him to dine if he turned up."

"You shut up, my son!" commanded Jake with absolute serenity. "It's not any business of yours anyway. We'll send you to bed before dinner if you aren't mighty careful."

Bunny laughed at the threat, but his sallow, boyish face coloured sensitively.

Saltash also laughed.

"Oh, you needn't do that, Jake. I'm as harmless as any dove, I assure you. You'll have to put up with me now. When shall I come?"

"Come tonight!" said Jake with quiet decision. "Eight o'clock if that suits you. Afraid I must go now. Bunny, take His Lordship to see Prince Charlie!"

He lifted a hand in salute and turned away, a man of no pretensions, either social or intellectual,

yet who knew how to hold his own with high and
low alike.

"Keeps you in order still, does he?" gibed Saltash as he watched him go. "You're getting too old
to be on a leading-string, *mon cher*."

Bunny frowned at the careless words.

"You don't know him. He's not that sort of
ass. We're pals, Jake and I, and I'm proud of it."

"Of course you are!" said Saltash comfortably.
"Didn't I tell you long ago that he was a gentleman? It's the way he's made. Hewn out of raw
material, but the real thing, and no mistake. You
must never quarrel with him on my account, Bunny, my lad. It would be very poor economy on
your part."

"I shan't do that," said Bunny. "But he's got
to do you justice. Maud says the same."

Saltash laughed aloud.

"But, my dear chap, nobody ever does that!
I don't myself!"

Bunny looked at him with affection.

"You always have tried to make yourself out a
worse rotter than you really are, haven't you, Charlie? I always tell Jake so."

"No, it's not my doing," said Saltash lightly.
"That's the rest of the world, *mon ami*. They like
their pictures highly coloured. So *pourquoi pas?*"

He snapped his fingers and laughed, and they
passed on together with careless jesting and friendly
chaff.

*   *   *

When Saltash arrived that evening he found
Bunny and Jake sauntering together in the sunset

glow along the gravelled terrace in front of the house.

He shot towards them in his car with that characteristic suddenness of his, swerving and coming to a stand before the porch with the confident ease of an alighting bird.

And here, seated in the porch and screened by white clematis, he found Maud, Jake's wife.

She rose to greet him, her eyes alight with pleasure.

"Oh, Charlie. I have wanted to shake hands with you ever since I heard of your escape."

He bent and kissed the hand she gave him.

"Gracious as ever! Had you begun to wear mourning for me, I wonder? It was a very cold bath, I assure you. We didn't enjoy it, any of us."

"I am sure you didn't. And you lost your yacht too! That was desperately unlucky."

"I am past the age for crying over spilt milk, Maud of the Roses."

He uttered his old name for her with daring assurance. "I have had worse losses than that in my time."

"And still you smile," she said. "A smile can conceal so much."

He turned to his host as he came up behind him.

"Well, Jake, I've taken you at your word, you see, and intruded into your virtuous household. How are Eileen and Molly and Betty and—last but not least—the son and heir?"

"Well done, Charlie!" Maud laughed softly. "How clever of you to remember them all!"

"Oh, yes, I am quite clever," said Saltash as again his hand met Jake's. "Too clever sometimes. I needn't ask if all goes well with you, Jake. Your prosperity is obvious, but don't wax fat on it! Bunny, now, he's as lean as a giraffe. Can't you do something to him? He looks as if he'd melt into thin air at a touch."

"Oh, don't be an ass!" protested Bunny. "I'm as strong as a horse anyway. Jake, tell him not to be an ass!"

"No good, I'm afraid," said Jake with his sudden smile. "Come inside, My Lord! The children are all flourishing but in bed at the present moment. The baby . . ."

"Oh, I must see the baby!" declared Saltash, turning back to Maud.

She laid a hand on his arm.

"I will take you to see him after dinner."

"Will you?" He smiled into her eyes. "I shall like that. But I shall probably want to shoot Jake when I come down again. Think it's a safe?"

She smiled back at him with confidence.

"Yes, I think so. Anyhow, I'm not afraid."

"Come and eat!" said Jake.

When dinner was over and Maud rose, Saltash sprang to open the door for her with that royal *bonhomie* of his which somehow gave him the right to enter where others waited for permission.

"Take Bunny with you!" he murmured. "I want to talk to Jake."

She lifted her eyes with a flash of surprise. He bent towards her.

"And afterwards to you, Queen Rose. I shall not forget to claim my privileges in that respect."

She laughed a little, but she obeyed his behest as a matter of course.

"Come for a turn in the garden with me, Bunny! I've hardly seen you today."

The boy got up, passing Jake with a careless slap on the shoulder that testified to the excellent good fellowship that existed between them.

Saltash turned back into the room and threw himself down by his host.

"That's right," he said as the door closed upon the brother and sister. "Now we can talk. There are several things I've come to consult you about, Jake."

"I'm listening," Jake answered.

"It's to do with young Bunny. What are you going to do with him?"

Jake leaned back and smoked for several seconds in silence. Saltash watched him with semi-comic curiosity.

"Something of a problem, eh?" he said after a pause.

He considered the matter for a few moments then slowly took the cigar from between his lips and spoke.

"It's certainly true; Bunny is a problem. He's not strong; and though he's got grit, he hasn't got what I call punching power."

"What I have to offer him is the post of bailiff at Burchester Castle, as old Bishop has got beyond his job," Saltash said. "I can't turn the old beggar out, but I want a young man to take the burden off his shoulders. Do you think that sort of thing would be beneath Bunny's dignity or likely to upset his morals?"

"He'll probably jump at the chance," Jake replied.

"Which is more than his worthy brother-in-law does on his behalf," grinned Saltash.

"No," Jake's steady eyes met the gibe unfalteringly. "I know it's a chance that doesn't come every day, and I know you mean well by him. I shan't put any hindrance in the way."

"Then it's done," said Saltash. "Bunny's fate is sealed."

"And where will he live?" Jake asked.

"With the old Bishops, of course. He'll be safe enough with them and within reach of you and Maud at the same time. It's time you eased the leading-string a bit, you know. He'll start kicking if you don't."

"I don't think so," said Jake. "He goes his own way already quite as much as is good for him. I don't need to hold him in very tight either. He's not the bolting sort."

"You mean you've trained him well," laughed Saltash. "I congratulate you. You've a genius for that sort of thing, Jake. The boy will probably answer to your lightest touch and never even know he does it."

Saltash paused a moment and then went on:

"You know Larpent, my captain, quite one of the best?"

Jake nodded. "I've met him—yes."

"He was damaged when the yacht went down. He's in a nursing home in town, getting better. He's got a daughter, a girl called Antoinette. She's been at school in France, and Larpent was bringing her home in the yacht when we went down.

"She's nineteen, a jolly little thing, half French. Larpent doesn't know what to do with her. He has no people. She, quite properly, wants to earn her own living. But she's too young yet to fight the world. Larpent's a rover, he'll never settle on land.

"She's never had any home life, poor kid. And she wants it. You'll say it's like my damned cheek to come to you, but on my life you and Maud are the only people I can think of."

The jerky utterance came to an end. Saltash turned his head towards Jake, watching him half furtively through the smoke.

There followed a silence of some duration. Jake's brows were slightly drawn. He spoke at last, slowly and softly as his manner was.

"Are you suggesting that Captain Larpent's daughter should come to us?"

"She'd be useful enough," said Saltash in his quick, vehement way. "She'd help Maud with the children. There's nothing she wouldn't do. It would be a kindness on your part, and you wouldn't regret it.

"She's a taking little thing. I'd like you to have her for a month, and if you don't want to keep her after that—well—shunt her back on to Larpent. He'll be well by that time. If he isn't, I'll look after her till he is."

"Who's looking after her now?" said Jake. "Where is she?"

Saltash pushed back his chair with a movement of impatience.

"Did you think I'd bring her to Burchester for all the county to blab about? She's under my protection, and she's safe."

He spoke with a certain fierceness and in a moment was pacing the room, his face arrogantly lifted.

"I know very well the sort of story that's going round, but if you're a white man you'll help me to give it the lie. I know I'm a blackguard, Jake, never pretended to be anything else. But I hope I'm a gentleman as well, at least where women are concerned. That child is none the worse in mind or body for being thrown on my hands. You've got to believe that."

"All right," said Jake.

Saltash paced jerkily on, his hands behind him.

"I want you to have her because you're straight, and she'll come to no harm with you. Will you take her, like a good chap, till something else safe turns up?"

Jake sat slowly forward.

"I'll have to talk it over with Maud."

Saltash's grip shifted impatiently.

"You know very well what Maud will say. Don't be an ass about it! Say 'No' if you mean to say 'No'—at once!"

There came the quiet tread of approaching feet on the gravelled terrace and the sound of low voices talking together. Jake lifted his head. His face was grim. He looked Saltash straight in the eyes.

"You've told me the plain truth about her? You swear it?"

Saltash's swarthy countenance was in shadow, but those strange eyes of his gleamed oddly, with the sort of fitful shining that comes from a coat of mail in an uncertain light.

They did not flinch from Jake's straight regard neither did they wholly meet it.

"Is my oath really more valuable than my word, Jake?" he said with a wry twist of the lips. "Most people don't find it so."

Jake stood up, a figure square and forceful. For a moment he faced Saltash with a level scrutiny that, possibly, pierced the coat of mail. Then abruptly he smiled.

"I will take your word, My Lord."

"And the child?" said Saltash.

Jake nodded. "The child too, if Maud agrees."

"Thanks," said Saltash and smiled back at Jake. "I am obliged to you, Jake. I think Maud will agree."

"Shall we go to her?" Jake asked.

They joined the two on the terrace and presently they were all laughing together at Saltash's drolleries. He knew how to bring effervescence to the very quietest waters.

Then after a while Jake strolled away for his nightly inspection of the Stables, taking Bunny with him, and Saltash and Maud were left alone.

He moved close to her at once, his arm stretched behind her along the back of the seat. At their feet lay an old red setter, Chops, who had belonged to Jake before his marriage and had devoted himself to Maud ever since.

He then told her about Toby, and she was delighted at the idea of looking after her.

"Then I may send that child to you tomorrow?" he asked.

"Why not bring her?" said Maud, smiling.

He shook his head.

"No. I'll come over one day, on Sunday, perhaps, and see you all again. I won't handicap her by bringing her."

They went into the drawing-room.

"Let's have some music!" he said and dropped

down before Maud's piano. "You are tired, *ma chère*. You shall listen."

He began to play an old French chanson that once they had sung together, and Maud leaned back on a deep settee near him and dreamily surrendered herself to its charm.

Charlie's touch had always been sheer delight to her. It held her now with the old sweet spell. His spirit spoke to hers with an intimacy which ordinary converse had never attained.

It was by his music that he first had spoken to her soul. In music they were always in complete accord.

She was half asleep in her corner with the old dog lying at her feet when Jake and Bunny came in, and Saltash very swiftly, with muffled chords, brought his performance to an end.

He sprang to his feet.

"I've been making love to your wife, Jake," he said, "and she has been heroically but quite ineffectually trying to keep me at a distance. I'd better go before I'm kicked out, eh?"

"Don't go on my account!" said Jake.

Saltash's brows twitched comically.

"Generous as ever! But I'm a rotten villain, Jake. I never could keep it up, and your virtuous presence is the last straw. Good-bye—and many thanks!"

He held Maud's hand in his right and stretched his left to Jake with a smile half whimsical and half derisive.

"There's nothing like banking on The Hundredth Chance," he said. "I shall try it myself one of these days."

"Say!" said Jake in his soft drawl. "I wish you luck!"

Saltash laughed and turned away, to be instantly seized upon by Bunny.

"I say, you are a good chap! The boss has been telling me. You're going to put me up to a job."

"If you'll take it," said Saltash.

Bunny thrust a hand through his arm and squeezed it impulsively.

"I'll take anything from you, Charlie. Hope I shall be man enough for you, that's all."

"Oh, you're man enough," said Saltash kindly. "Just the sort I want. Look here, I can't stop now. But I'll come over on Sunday and talk things over—if Jake permits."

"Any day," said Jake.

Saltash nodded. "Good. I'll ring you up tomorrow, Maud. You're sure you mean tomorrow?"

"Quite sure," she said with a smile.

He swept her a bow and went out with Bunny.

*   *   *

The following day Maud remained in bed as she had a violent headache.

She lay in her darkened room too battered to think, while with characteristic decision Jake assumed the direction of the household, provoking unwilling admiration from Mrs. Lovelace, the housekeeper, who was somewhat given to disparage men as "poor things who never did a hand's turn for 'emselves if they could get the women to do it for 'em."

One of Jake's horses was running at Graydown that afternoon, and at the end of the morning he returned to the house for a hasty lunch before leaving for the racecourse.

All memory of Saltash's *protégée* had left him, but it returned to his mind as he saw the extra place laid at the table.

He looked at his watch and realized that she ought to have arrived half an hour before. Bunny was also absent, presumably waiting for her.

He paid Maud a brief visit before departing and found her better. She was half dressed and lying on a couch in her room.

He extracted a promise from her that she would not go down before tea, though she demurred somewhat on the score of the expected visitor.

"Leave her to Bunny!" said Jake. "He's quite capable of looking after her for an hour or two."

"I think Bunny meant to go to the races," she said.

"Well, he can't for once." Jake frowned. "Don't you fret now! She'll be all right."

"Well, tell them to bring her straight up to see me when she arrives!" Maud begged him. "I shan't be asleep, and really I am much better."

"All right," he replied. "I'll do that."

Her thoughts turned dreamily to Saltash. What a pity he did not find some nice girl to marry!

"If only some decent woman would fall in love with him!" She sighed and then found herself smiling wistfully at the thought that Saltash's heart would not be an easy thing to capture.

He was far too accustomed to adulation wherever he went.

"Besides, he's such a flirt," she reflected. "One never knows whether he is in earnest till the mischief is done."

It was nearly two hours later that she became somewhat suddenly aware of feet sauntering under her window and young voices talking together.

"Hullo!" said one abruptly; it was Bunny's, speaking with careless friendliness. "Stand still a minute! There's an immense green caterpillar waving to me from your hat-brim."

A voice that was like a boy's, clear, bell-like, instantly replied:

"Oh, hell! Do take it off!"

Maud started wide awake with involuntary shrinking.

There came a chuckle from Bunny and, after a pause and the eloquent crunch of a heel on the gravel, his voice on a note of laughter.

"I didn't say it!"

"Great Scott!" ejaculated the clear boyish tones. "Do you mean you're shocked?"

"Not at all," said Bunny courteously.

"Well, then, what does it matter who said it?" demanded the other.

"It doesn't matter," said Bunny, still suppressing merriment. "Except that it isn't said in this house."

"Oh, damn!" said the newcomer disconsolately. "Then I shall soon be sent back in disgrace."

"Cheer up!" said Bunny. "We don't convict on a first offence as a rule in this country."

"But I shall never remember!" groaned the other, and for the first time the words held a note that was not wholly boyish; it sounded wistful, even rather piteous. "People's ways are all so different.

It's rather infernal, trying to please everybody, you know, Bunny."

"Never mind!" said Bunny in a brotherly tone. "I'll kick you every time I see it coming if you like."

"Will you really? That would be jolly decent of you."

The wistfulness vanished in a laugh that was quick and musical, wholly spontaneous.

"You bet I will!" said Bunny.

"Right-O! Mind you do! Now get out of the way and see me jump that rose-tree!"

There followed a light scamper of feet, and Maud raised herself swiftly and leaned forth in time to see an athletic little figure in navy blue, wearing a jaunty Panama hat, skim like a bird over a sweeping Dorothy Perkins and alight on one leg with the perfect poise of a winged Mercury on the other side.

Bunny's lanky form followed and also cleared the rose-tree with infinitely less grace, and again the girl laughed, her wide blue eyes alight with mirth.

"What an antic! I thought you were going to pull up the rose-bush with your heels! What are you doing that for?"

Bunny's hands were on her shoulders. He was plainly enjoying himself thoroughly.

"I'm feeling for the wings," he explained. "I'll swear you never jumped it. Where do you keep 'em?"

She drew herself away from his touch.

"No, I haven't got any. They don't grow on people like me. Don't let's stay here! I feel as if we're being watched."

It was then that Maud spoke from her window

in her quiet, gentle voice that yet held a certain authority.

"Bunny, bring our visitor up to see me!"

Both Bunny and his companion started and looked up, and Maud saw the girl's face fully for the first time, a nervous little face with haunting, wide blue eyes made more intense by the short, thick black lashes that surrounded them, eyes that seemed to plead for kindness.

There was charm about the pointed chin and a good deal of sweetness about the moulding of the mouth.

But it was the eyes that held Maud's attention. They were the eyes of a creature who has known the wild agony of fear and is not easily reassured.

Yet the face was the face of a child.

She leaned out a little further on her sill and addressed the stranger.

"Come up and speak to me!" she said very kindly. "Bunny will show you the way."

A shy flickering smile answered her. She cast a questioning look at Bunny.

"Yes, that's Maud—my sister," said Bunny. "Come along! This way!"

They entered the house by a French window and Maud drew back into her room. What was there in that childish face that appealed so tremendously to her womanhood, wholly banishing her first involuntary sense of recoil?

She could not have said; she was only conscious of the woman in her throbbing with a deep compassion.

She stood and waited for the child's coming with a strangely poignant expectation.

She heard Bunny's voice talking cheerily on

the stairs, but his words provoked no response. She went to the door and opened it.

Bunny was leading the way; in fact his companion seemed to be lagging very considerably in the rear.

Maud moved out into the passage, and Bunny stood to one side with a courteous gesture.

"*Mademoiselle* Antoinette Larpent!" he announced.

The small figure in blue drew itself together with a certain bravado and came forward.

Maud held out her hands.

"My dear child, I expected you long ago."

The hands she clasped were very small and cold. They did not cling to her as she had half expected. The blue eyes flashed her a single nervous glance and fell.

"I'm sorry I'm late, Madam," said the visitor in a low, punctilious voice.

Maud felt amused and chilled in the same moment.

"Come and sit down! We will have some tea upstairs. Bunny, go and order it, will you?"

"With pleasure," said Bunny. "And may I return?"

She smiled at him as she passed an arm about the girl's narrow shoulders.

"Yes, you can come back when it's ready. Come in here, dear! You will like to take off your things. How long have you been here?"

"Only five minutes," came the murmured answer; she thought it had a deprecating sound.

"You must be tired," she said kindly. "You came from town? How is it you are so late? Did you miss your train?"

"No, Madam." Very nervously came the reply.

The contrast between this and the boyish freedom of manner on the terrace a few seconds before would have been ludicrous if it had not been somehow pathetic.

She passed on, too considerate to press for details.

"Take off your hat and coat, won't you? When we have had some tea I will take you to your room."

She was pleased to see that Charlie's *protégée* was garbed with extreme simplicity. Her fair hair, which had been closely shorn, was beginning to curl at the ends.

She liked the delicate contrasting line of the black brows above the deep blue of the eyes. She noticed that the veins on the white temples showed with great distinctness.

"Sit down!" she said. "And now you must tell me what to call you. Your name is Antoinette, isn't it?"

"I'm generally called Toby," said the visitor in a very shy voice. "But you will call me . . . what you like."

"Would you like me to call you Toby?" Maud asked.

"Yes, please," said Toby with unexpected briskness.

"Very well, my dear," Maud smiled. "Then that is settled. We are not going to be strangers, you and I. I expect you know that Lord Saltash and I are great friends, though I have never met your father."

Toby's pale young face flushed suddenly. She was silent for a moment.

"Lord Saltash has been very good to me," she said in her shy voice. "He . . . saved me from drowning. Wasn't it . . . wasn't it nice of him to . . . take the trouble?"

"Quite nice of him," Maud agreed. "You must have been very frightened, weren't you?"

Toby suppressed a shudder. .

"I was rather. And the water was dreadfully cold. I thought we should never come up again. It was like . . . it was like . . ."

She stopped herself.

"He said I was never to talk about it . . . or think about it . . . so I won't, if you don't mind."

"Tell me about your father!" said Maud sympathetically.

For the second time the blue eyes flashed towards her.

"Oh, he is still ill in a nursing home and not allowed to see anyone."

There was a hint of recklessness in her voice.

"They say he'll get well again, but . . . I don't know."

"You are anxious about him," Maud said.

"No, I'm not." Recklessness became something akin to defiance. "I don't like him much. He's so surly."

"My dear!" said Maud, momentarily disconcerted.

"Well, it's no good pretending I do when I don't, is it?" said Toby, and suddenly smiled at her with winning gracelessness. "It isn't my fault. We're not friends, never have been."

She made a little gesture of the hands.

"Why, we hardly know each other. I'd never been on *The Night Moth* before."

"And you'll never go again," commented Bunny, entering at the moment. "Maud, do you know I took Miss Larpent . . ." he turned deliberately to Toby, who snapped her fingers in airy acknowledgement, "to see the races instead of coming straight back, according to the boss's instructions?"

"Oh! So that's where you've been!" said Maud.

"Exactly so."

Bunny pulled up a chair and disposed his long legs astride it.

"We saw several events and made a bit. Then Forest Fire let us down badly and we lost the lot. After that we went into the paddock to cool ourselves and met the boss, who at once, somewhat rudely, ordered us home.

"I have an impression he's feeling waxy with me for some reason," Bunny ended, stroking his chin reflectively. "Daresay I shall get over it, however."

"What a pity you went!" said Maud.

"Not at all," said Bunny. "We enjoyed it. It's fun doing naughty things sometimes, isn't it—er—Miss Larpent?"

"Don't be an ass!" said Toby tersely.

Maud raised her brows, but Bunny grinned with delight.

"Thank you, Toby! I take the hint. There shall be no more ceremony between us. Ah! There come the children along the path by the summer-house!"

He sprang to the window and sent forth a yell, turning back almost instantly to say:

"Sorry, Maud! I'm afraid I forgot your head. How is it?"

He did not wait for her reply but leaned out again immediately to address the advancing children with noisy gaiety.

Toby looked up at Maud, hesitated, and rose.

"Let us go and have tea with the children! It will be quieter for you."

Maud put out a gentle hand to her.

"No, dear. You stay with me. Bunny may, if he likes!"

This time Toby's fingers closed tightly upon her own.

"Sure?" Toby asked.

"Quite sure," said Maud, smiling at her.

Toby turned sharply and pinched Bunny's elbow as he leaned from the window. He drew himself in and stared at her.

"You're making too much noise," she told him curtly. "You go and racket downstairs!"

Bunny's eyes widened for a second in indignant amazement, then abruptly he threw up his chin and laughed.

"I like you! You're the corkiest thing in girls I've ever seen!"

Toby pulled at his elbow like a small, persistent dog.

"Go on! Go down to them! Mrs. Bolton and I want to have our tea alone. I'll come and play with you presently if you're good."

It was spoken wholly without coquetry, much as an elder brother might speak to a younger. It was plain that she meant to have her way, thought Maud. She knew that there was a very strong mixture of stubbornness in Bunny and wondered if she would get it.

Amusement, however, kept the upper hand with him. Toby's treatment evidently appealed strongly to his sense of humour.

Perhaps her determination also made its impression upon him, for after a little more chaff on his part and brisk insistence on hers he departed, laughing, to join the children.

Toby saw him to the door and returned, calm and triumphant.

"Well done!" said Maud. "You know how to deal with spoilt children evidently."

Toby looked at her sharply as she sat down, almost as if she suspected a double meaning to the words.

"Do you mean men?" she said, for an instant her childish face wore a look of contempt. "Oh, anyone can manage men, given a fair chance. There's not much cleverness needed for that."

She spoke with the decision of one who knew, and in spite of the difference of years between them Maud could not question her confidence.

She had a curious feeling that either by experience or intuition this girl knew more than she.

She made no comment, therefore, and after a moment Toby spoke her last word on the subject with characteristic brevity.

"There's only one rule to follow with men . . . that is, if you want any peace at all. Make up your mind and stick to it! If they don't like it, let 'em go to . . ."

She checked suddenly and coloured deeply under Maud's eyes.

"I mean, let 'em do the other thing!" she ended on a note that somehow seemed to ask for pardon.

"I see," said Maud gently in a tone that conveyed it.

Toby threw her a little smile, half grateful and half mischievous; and curiously in that moment a bond was formed between them which was destined to endure.

Chapter
Four

"Well?" said Saltash with quizzical interest. "Where is she? And how is she getting on?"

It was the Sunday afternoon of his promised visit, a day soft with spring flowers and fleeting sunshine. Maud sat in a basket-chair on the verandah and regarded him with puzzled eyes.

She passed his question by.

"Charlie," she said, "where does she come from?"

He raised his shoulders expressively.

"Where do all women come from—and why, *chère reine?* It would be such a peaceful planet without them."

He was in a baffling mood and she knew better than to pursue the subject under those conditions. She abandoned her effort with a sigh.

"She is not a woman; she is a child, very charming but utterly irresponsible. She is in the training-field just now with Jake and Bunny. She is a positive delight to Jake. She can do anything with the horses."

"But not such a delight to you?" suggested Saltash shrewdly.

Maud hesitated momentarily.

"I love her, of course. But ... though I have tried to make her feel at ease, I think she is a little afraid of me, afraid anyhow to be quite natural in my presence."

"But are we any of us that?" protested Saltash. "Are we not all on our best behaviour in the audience-chamber?"

"They are all great pals," she said irrelevantly. "She and Bunny are terribly reckless. I hope they won't break their necks before they have done."

"Or their hearts?" suggested Saltash, looking mischievous.

"I don't think there is much danger of that anyhow at present." She smiled. "She is a positive child, Charlie, as young as Eileen in many ways, or perhaps younger. Shall we walk down to the field and look at them?"

"Your servant!" said Saltash readily.

He was on his feet in an instant, and she realized that he had been chaffing to go since the moment of his arrival.

"You take a great interest in her," she remarked as they walked along the terrace.

He made his most appalling grimace.

"I have never had an infant to look after before. And I have to make my report to Larpent."

"How is he?" questioned Maud.

He shot her a swift glance.

"Is the child anxious?"

"Not in the least. I don't believe she ever

thinks about him. She told me on the first day that
she hardly knows him."

"How honest of her!" Saltash laughed. "Well,
he's getting better, but he won't be well yet. May I
leave her in your charge a while longer?"

"Of course!" Maud said warmly. "I love to
have her, and she is a great help to me too. The
children simply worship her, and she is splendid
with them. I believe Eileen will very soon get over
her dread of riding."

"Toby can ride?" Saltash asked.

"Oh, yes, like a cowboy. She is amazingly fearless and never minds a tumble in the least. She can
do the most extraordinary things exactly like a boy.
I am always afraid of her coming to grief, but she
never does."

"Funny little beggar!" Saltash laughed.

"I am quite sure of one thing," pursued Maud.
"She never learnt those things at any school. She
tells me she has been to a good many."

"I believe that's true," said Saltash. "I imagine
she is fairly quick to pick up anything, but I haven't
known her myself for long."

"She must have picked up a good deal on *The
Night Moth*," observed Maud unexpectedly.

He glanced at her again.

"Why do you say that? She was under my protection and Larpent's on *The Night Moth*."

"I know. She idolizes you."

Maud smiled at him somewhat dubiously.

"But she must have mixed fairly freely with
the crew to have picked up the really amazing language she sometimes uses."

Saltash's brows worked whimsically.

"Some of us have a gift that way. Your worthy Jake, for instance . . ."

"Oh, Jake is a reformed character," she interrupted. "He hardly ever lets himself go nowadays. And he won't allow it from Bunny. But Toby . . . Toby never seems to know the good from the bad."

"Has Jake taken her in hand?" asked Saltash with a chuckle.

"Oh, yes. He checks her at every turn. I must say she takes it very sweetly, even offered to take her meals in her room yesterday when he was rather down on her. It absolutely disarmed Jake, of course. What could he say?"

"Yes, she is a disarming monkey, certainly," agreed Saltash. "But I never was great on the management and discipline of children. So she knocks under to the great Jake, does she?"

"Oh, not entirely," Maud laughed a little. "Only this morning they had a battle. I don't know how it is going to end yet. But she can be very firm."

"She never tried any battles with me," said Saltash with some complacence.

"No. But then your sense of duty is more elastic than Jake's. You never probably asked her to do anything she didn't want to do."

"Can't remember," said Saltash. "What did Jake want?"

"You'll laugh, of course." Maud smiled. "But Jake is quite right, whatever you do. He wanted her to go to church with little Eileen and me this morning. She's only a child, you know, and he naturally took it for granted that she was going.

"We both did. But just at the last moment she

absolutely refused, told him quite frankly that she was an atheist."

Saltash's laugh had a sound, half mocking, half exultant.

"What did the worthy Jake say to that? Stop! I know what he said. He said, 'You can call yourself by any fool name you please, but you've got to go to church like a respectable citizen if I say so.' Wasn't that it?"

"Something like that," Maud admitted. "How did you know?"

"Oh, I know Jake," said Saltash drily. "And what happened then? She refused?"

"Yes, she refused. She was frightened, but she refused. She looked as if she were going to run away, but in the end Jake went off with her to the Stables, saying they would go tonight.

"They were quite friends when I saw them again, but she had been crying, poor little thing. I wish I could help her, but somehow I can't get near enough. Jake seems to understand her best."

"Wonder if she will give in," Saltash murmured.

"I don't think there is much doubt about that." Maud smiled.

Saltash laughed again mockingly.

"Oh, we all know Jake is invincible, virtuous rectitude incarnate. But you can't hammer a girl into submission like a boy, and I rather fancy that Toby is not wholly ignorant of the art of getting her own way."

"Jake never hammered Bunny," Maud said quietly. "But he manages him."

They rounded a curve and came upon the

gate that led into the field. The galloping hoofs
were close to them. As they reached the corner two
riders flashed past at full speed. One of them, Bunny,
lay on his horse's neck, yelling wild encouragement
to his mount.

The other, a slight, childish figure, was kneeling on the saddle like a small, crouching creature,
perfectly posed and wholly unafraid.

As the horse that carried her dropped to a
canter on the hill, she got to her feet with absolute
ease and stood, arms out and swaying to the animal's motion, till, as they rounded another curve,
she dropped to the saddle again and passed from
sight, following in Bunny's tracks.

"Quite a pretty exhibition!" remarked Saltash.
"Where is Jake?"

Jake himself appeared at the moment, riding
soberly, mounted on his favourite horse, The Hundredth Chance.

He greeted Saltash with a smile and jumped to
the ground to join them at the gate.

"They'll be round again directly. Just riding off
their spirits," he explained in his easy drawl. "You
motored over, My Lord?"

Saltash nodded with a touch of impatience.
He was watching with restless eyes for the reappearance of the girl on horseback. She had not
seen him at the gate, yet somehow his arrogance
rebelled at the fact that she had passed him by.

Jake stood with The Hundredth Chance nuz-
zling against him. He did not trouble himself to
make conversation; that was not his way. He also
waited for the reappearance of the riders.

They came riding side by side and jesting with

careless *camaraderie*. Toby's face was delicately
flushed. The fair head had no covering. She was
dressed and looked exactly like a boy.

At sight of Saltash standing by the gate her
whole attitude changed. She uttered a queer sound,
half whoop, half sob, and flung herself out of the
saddle.

In a moment she had reached him, was hanging
to his arm in mute greeting, everything else in the
world forgotten. It was pathetically like the reunion
of a lost dog to its master.

Saltash's face softened miraculously at her action. The jest died on his lips.

"Why, Nonette! Nonette!"

She strangled another sob. Her face was burning, quivering, appealing, no longer the face of a
boy.

"I thought you'd forgotten to come."

"What? Was I expected to lunch?" said Saltash. "Ah! Was that why you wouldn't go to
church?"

Toby looked up, desperately smiling.

"It may have been . . . partly. But I never do
go. Do you?"

"Not often," said Saltash. "I might if I stayed
here. There's no knowing. You'll be pleased to
hear your daddy is better. He's coming down to the
Castle to convalesce. And when he's done that I'm
going to have a party, a coming-out party for you."

"For me!" Toby gasped, staring at him with
scared blue eyes. "I hope you won't, Sir."

He laughed back at her, his brows working
mischievously.

"Mais pourquoi pas, mignonne?" You are old
enough. Maud will come and be hostess, won't you,

Maud? You shall have Jake too, for a watchdog, if you want him.

"After that you shall be presented at Court, when you've learnt to curtsy prettily instead of turning somersaults. You must let your hair grow, Nonette, and leave off wearing breeks. You've got to be a credit to me."

"Oh, damn!" said Toby in dismay. "I mean ... oh, bother!"

"Yes, it's a good thing you mean only that, isn't it?" Saltash laughed. "If you go on wearing those masculine things much longer, you'll have Jake punching your head for little slips of that kind. He's getting mighty particular, I'm told."

"Not afraid of Jake!" said Toby, casting a swift look at her host.

Jake was lighting his pipe. His face wore a faint smile. He was holding Toby's animal as well as his own.

"Aren't you going to ride again?"

"No," said Toby.

"Oh, come on!" Bunny pushed his horse forward without dismounting. "Glad to see you, Charlie, but we must have one more gallop. Come on, Toby! Be a sport!"

But Toby, still holding Saltash's sleeve, would not so much as look at him.

"Not coming."

Saltash laughed.

Bunny coloured suddenly and hotly.

"Oh, all right!" he said and, wheeling his horse, rode away.

"Now you've hurt his feelings," observed Saltash.

"Who cares?" said Toby and nestled closer till

with his sudden reckless grin he thrust an arm about her shoulders.

"I'll tell you what it is, Nonette. You're getting spoilt all round. Something will have to be done. Shall I take her away, Jake?"

"And bring me back when I'm good?" put in Toby eagerly.

He laughed and pinched her ear.

"I shall want to keep you myself, when you're good. I haven't yet found anyone to sew on buttons like you do. No, *ma chère*, you'll have to stay and be caned for your sins. Jake is a better schoolmaster than I am, being so eminently virtuous himself. I hope you do cane her, Jake. I'm sure she needs it."

"No," Jake said, preparing to mount again. "I haven't tried that at present."

Toby watched him a little wistfully as he moved away, leading her horse.

"I am trying to be good. He knows that."

"Yes, she's trying hard," Maud said very kindly. "Jake and I are going to be proud of her some day."

Saltash's brows twisted humorously.

"I wonder!"

And then again lightly he laughed.

"Don't get too good, Nonette! I can't rise to that."

She turned swiftly, looking up into the derisive face above her with open adoration in her own.

"You!" she said. "You!"

"Well, what about me?" he asked.

She coloured very deeply.

"Nothing, Sir, nothing! Only . . . you're so great!"

He flicked her cheek, grimacing hideously.

"Is that your pretty way of telling me I'm the biggest rotter you ever met?"

"Oh, no!" said Toby quickly and earnestly. "Oh, no! I think you are . . . a king! If . . . if any-one could make me believe in God, you could."

She spoke with a sincerity that held a hint of passion. The grimace flicked out of Saltash's face like a picture from a screen. For a moment he had the blank look of a man who has been hit, he knows not where.

Then with lightning swiftness his eyes went to Maud.

"You hear that?" he said, almost on a note of challenge. "Why don't you laugh?"

She met his look with absolute steadfastness. There was a certain pity in her own.

"Because," she said with great gentleness, "I believe that it is true."

In the silence that followed she waited for his own laugh of mockery and did not hear it. The odd eyes comprehended her and passed her by, fell abruptly to Toby and dwelt upon her with a whim-sical tenderness.

"I always said you were a little ass, didn't I, Toby?"

And Toby turned with an apologetic murmur and softly kissed his hand.

* * *

Toby went to church that Sunday evening with great propriety, Saltash having departed, taking Bunny with him to spend the evening at Burchester.

Her behaviour was a model of decorum throughout.

When they returned home, Maud went to the piano and Toby came and sat on a low chair near her and listened in absolute stillness while she played.

They were alone and Maud played on and on, almost forgetful of her silent companion, suffering her fingers to wander in unison with her thoughts. All her life music had been her great joy and solace.

She was not a brilliant musician as was Saltash, but she had the gift of so steeping herself in music that she could at times thereby express that which otherwise would have been unutterable, the hidden emotions of her soul.

Nearly an hour had passed thus before she remembered the silent little figure behind her, and then it was with a swift sense of compunction that she took her hands from the keys and turned.

"Toby, dear, how boring this must be for you! Are you asleep? Why, child, what is it?"

With a start she saw that Toby's fair head was bowed upon her arms in an attitude of the most hopeless, the most bitter, despair.

She made a convulsive movement at the sound of Maud's voice and in a moment lifted a white, strained face.

"I am just a little tired, that's all," she said in a voice that quivered in spite of her. "Please go on playing! I like it."

Maud got up with quiet decision and went to her, but Toby was on her feet before she reached her. She stood with that look of a small, frightened animal so characteristic of her, her two hands nervously locked together.

Maud took her gently by the arm.

"Shall we sit down and talk?"

Toby yielded as it were involuntarily to the quiet touch. In her plain white blouse with the sailor collar she looked a mere child, a piteous, shy child.

Maud drew her down upon the sofa. All the mother in her went out to the forlorn little creature, yet for the moment she hesitated, as one afraid to strike a wrong note.

Toby was trembling a little and that fact decided her. She put a comforting arm about her.

"Do you know, I am wondering how to make you happy."

"You are very kind and I am stupid . . . stupid." Toby choked back a sob. "I will try to be happy. I will, really."

Maud began to draw her gently nearer, but Toby surprised her by a sudden, passionate movement and slipped down on to the floor, hiding her face against her.

"I'm not fit . . . to speak to you!" she said in a vehement, strangled whisper. "I'm so bad . . . so bad. And I do . . . so . . . want to be good."

"My dear, dear child!" Maud said very tenderly.

Toby fought with herself for a space, her thin arms tightly clasped Maud's knees. At last, forcing back her distress, she lifted her head.

"I'm so dreadfully sorry. Don't let it upset you! Don't . . . tell Jake!"

"You are quite safe with me, dear," Maud assured her. "But can't I help you?"

She knew even as she asked the question that Toby was not prepared to give her full confidence, and her own reserve shrank from asking for it.

Toby looked up at her with quivering lips.

"Oh, you are good! I want to be good . . . like you. But . . . I don't feel as if I ever shall be."

Maud laid a very gentle hand upon the blue-veined forehead.

"I think goodness is only comparative at the best of times. If I seem so to you, it is probably because my life holds very few temptations to be anything else."

"Ah!" Toby said with a quick sigh. "And do you think people ought to be made to suffer for . . . for things they can't help?"

Maud shook her head.

"I am afraid it often happens, dear."

"And yet you believe in God," Toby said.

"Yes, I believe in God. And I am quite sure, Toby, quite, quite sure that He never holds people responsible for the things they can't help."

"Then why . . . ?" began Toby restlessly.

"No, no! Don't ask why!" Maud interrupted her. "The world is as He made it. We are His workmanship. Let Him do with us as He will!"

Toby's hands clenched. A frown that was curiously unchildlike drew the wide forehead.

"Are we to be quite passive then? Just . . . slaves?"

"No," Maud said. "Servants, not slaves. There is a big difference. And every one of us, every one of us, has God's work to do in the world."

"And you think that bad people . . . like me . . . can do anything?" said Toby.

"Toby, dear, I am quite sure that your work is waiting for you." Maud smiled.

"Don't know where I'm going to begin," said Toby with another sigh.

"My dear, you have begun."

Maud's hand smoothed the fair hair.

"Do you think I don't know how hard you try?"

Toby's eyes filled with quick tears.

"But is it any good trying? Shall I ever get away from . . . from . . . ?"

She broke off with a nervous, upward glance.

"Shall I ever do more than begin?"

"My dear, yes."

Very quietly, with absolute decision, Maud answered.

"You are young, too young to be hampered by anything that is past. You have your life before you, and to a very great extent you can make of it what you will. There is no need, believe me, there is no need to look back.

"There is only time enough for the present. Just keep on trying! Make the very best you can of it! And you will find the future will come out all right."

"Will it?" said Toby rather dubiously.

Maud bent and kissed her.

"Certainly it will, dear. Never doubt it! It may not be the future we plan for ourselves, but it will be the very best possible if we keep on doing our best with the present."

"Thank you," Toby murmured gratefully. "And you really think . . . you do really think . . . the past doesn't matter?"

Maud was silent for a few moments. The thought of Saltash was in her mind, his jesting evasions, his air of careless proprietorship.

What was the thing in this child's past that she desired so earnestly to put away? She wondered if she ought to ask, but she could not.

A slight tremor ran through the small, suppli-
cating figure at her knee, and quick pity banished
doubt.

"I think it is entirely in our own hands, dear.
The past can always be left behind if we work
hard enough."

"Oh, thank you," Toby said again, and gathering Maud's hands impulsively into her own she
kissed them. "I'm going to work very hard. You'll
help me, I know. I've got to . . . to leave off turning somersaults . . . and learn to . . . curtsy."

She sent a shy smile into Maud's face, and almost in spite of herself Maud answered it.

There was something oddly appealing, irresistibly attractive, about the child. She was so young
and ardent yet so pathetically anxious to please.

"Of course I will help you," she said. "I will
always help you, my dear."

And Toby, emboldened, thrust warm arms
about her neck and held her close.

*   *   *

The perfect rose of a June sunset was slant-
ing through the fir-woods at Burchester Park, making the red trunks glow. At the end of a long grass
ride the new moon dipped to the west, a silver boat
uptilted in a green, transparent sea.

A very great stillness lay upon all things, the
eventide quiet of a summer day.

The dull thudding of a horse's hoofs along the
ride scarcely seemed to break that magic silence.
A frightened rabbit scurrying to cover made no
sound at all. Somewhere, a long way off, a cuckoo
was calling, tenderly, persistently. Somewhere, near
at hand, a blackbird was warbling to his mate.

But it all went into the enchanted silence, blending with the hush of the coming night. The man who rode the horse was conscious only of the peace of his surroundings. He doffed his cap to the moon in mock reverence and carried it in his hand.

He came to the end of the ride and checked his animal on the brow of a steep descent. The park lay below him wrapped in mystery. On another slope a full mile away stood the Castle, ancient, battlemented, starkly splendid, one westward-facing window burning as with fire.

He sat motionless for a space, gazing across at it, his face a curious mask of conjecture and regret.

Finally, with great suddenness, he lifted his hand and struck his horse sharply on the flank. In a moment he was being precipitated at a headlong gallop down the hill.

He went like the wind, and the enchanted wood was left behind.

Riding up the further slope to the Castle a few minutes later, he was hailed from behind and reined in to look back.

A long-legged figure detached itself from a clump of trees that shadowed the bailiff's house and came racing in pursuit.

"Hi! Charlie! Don't be in such a deuce of a hurry! I'm going your way."

Saltash waited not too patiently.

"My good chap, you're dressed and I'm not! I shall be late for my guests."

"What's it matter?" scoffed Bunny breathlessly, reaching his side. "Maud and Jake don't count, and Toby is only a kid. I don't suppose she's ever been out to dine before."

"She's old enough to begin," remarked Saltash, pushing on at a walk.

"Well, she is beginning," said Bunny with a grin as he strode beside him. "You haven't seen her for some weeks, have you? You'll see a difference and so will her father."

"How?" said Saltash briefly.

Bunny's grin became more pronounced.

"Oh, it's chiefly clothes. Maud is rather clever in that line, you know. I haven't seen a great deal of her lately. She's generally scampering round on horseback with Jake.

"But once or twice with Maud I've seen her look quite demure. She's really getting almost good-looking," he added dispassionately.

Saltash flung a swift look downwards.

"Don't you approve?"

Bunny shrugged his shoulders.

"I don't see enough of her to care either way. She's still a kid, you know—quite a kid."

Saltash dropped the subject abruptly.

"You're liking your job all right?"

"Rather!" Bunny replied enthusiastically. "It's just the sort of thing I was made for. Old Bishop's a brick. We're getting quite fond of one another."

"Sort of life you enjoy?" questioned Saltash.

"Oh, rather! I've always thought I'd like to manage a big estate. Wish I'd got one of my own."

"All right, I'll adopt you." Saltash laughed. "You shall be the son of my old age."

"Oh, don't be an ass!" protested Bunny. "Why on earth don't you get married?"

Saltash's brows twisted wryly.

"Afraid I've lived too long, *mon cher*. If I had

married your sister in the long ago, things might have been vastly different. As it is, I see no prospect of changing my state. Think it matters?"

"Well, it's rather a shame to let a good name die out," maintained Bunny. "And of course it's rot to talk like that about Maud. You can't pretend to have stayed in love with her all these years. There must have been heaps of others since then."

"No, I'm not pretending," said Saltash. "As you say, there have been heaps of others."

He made an odd gesture towards the western sky behind him.

"There are always heaps of stars, Bunny! But there's never more than one moon."

"Rot!" Bunny exclaimed.

"It is, isn't it?" said Saltash and laughed with brief derision. "Well, I must get on. You can do the receiving if I'm late. Tell them I've been in town and only got back at midday! You needn't bother about Larpent. I'll see to him."

He flicked his horse's neck and was off with the words.

* * *

Saltash approached the open door that led out upon the great staircase. He reached it and stretched out both hands with a fine gesture of greeting.

"Welcome to my poor hovel!" he said. "Madam, I kneel at your feet."

A clear, high laugh answered him from below, and both Larpent and Bunny turned sharply at the sound.

A figure in white, girlish, fresh as the morning, sprang suddenly into view. Her eager face had the delicate flush of a wild rose. The hair clustered about her temples in tender ringlets of gold.

Her eyes, blue and shining, gave her the look of a child just awakened from happy sleep, a child that expects to be lifted up and kissed.

"By Jove!" murmured Bunny under his breath, staring openly. "By Jove!"

And there words failed him. He had never been so astounded in his life. This girl, this funny little Toby with the sharp features and pointed chin, the girl-urchin with whom he had chaffed and played, was actually a beauty, and till that amazing moment he had not realized the fact.

As he went forward to greet her, he saw that Larpent was staring also, and he chuckled inwardly at the sight. Decidedly it must be a worse shock for Larpent than it was for himself, he reflected.

For at least he had seen her in the chrysalis stage, though most certainly he had never expected this wonderful butterfly to emerge.

Maud, of course, was the witch who had worked the marvellous transformation. Maud with her tender mother-wisdom that divined so much. He looked at her now and wondered, as he met her smile, if she fully realized what she had done.

Across the wonder came Saltash's quizzing voice.

"Mais Nonette, Nonette, you are a vision for the gods!"

And a curious hot pang that was like a physical stab went through Bunny. How dared Charlie use that caressing tone to her, as though she were a mere ordinary woman to be trifled with and cajoled?

He had never disapproved of Saltash before,

but for that moment he almost hated him. She was too young, too sweet, too different, to be treated thus.

And then he was standing close to her, and Saltash, laughing, pushed him forward.

"Do you know this fellow, *ma chère?*"

The wide blue eyes came up to his with a pleased smile of comradeship.

"Why, it's Bunny!" the clear voice said. "I'm so glad you're here too in this ogre's Castle."

Her hand gave his a little confiding squeeze, and Bunny's fingers gripped in answer. He realized suddenly that she was nervous, and all the ready chivalry of his nature rose up to protect her. For a moment or two he kept her hand close in his own.

Then Saltash airily took it from him.

"Come! Here is someone else you ought to know!"

He wheeled her round with the words. She came face to face with Larpent. There was an instant of dead silence, then Toby uttered a little quivering laugh.

"Hullo . . . Captain!" she said.

"Hullo!" said Larpent, paused a moment, then abruptly took her by the chin and, stooping, touched the wide brow with his lips. "All right?" he asked gruffly.

Toby gave a little gasp; she seemed to be trembling. But in a second she laughed again with more assurance.

"Yes, all right, Captain. I . . . I . . . I'm glad to see you again. You all right too?"

Bunny, looking on, made the abrupt discovery that Larpent also was embarrassed. It was Saltash who answered for him, covering the moment's awkwardness with the innate ease of manner which never seemed to desert him.

"Of course he's all right. Don't you worry about him! We're going to buy him another boat as soon as the insurance company have done talking. Maud, this is my captain, the finest yachtsman you've ever met and my very good friend."

He threw his merry, daredevil glance at Larpent as he made the introduction, and turned immediately to Jake, who had just entered.

"You two ought to get on all right. He disapproves of me almost as strongly as you do, and like you he endures me, he knows not why!"

Jake's red-brown eyes held a smile that made his rugged face look kindly as he replied.

"Maybe we both have the sense to spot a winner when we see one, My Lord."

Saltash's brows went up derisively.

"And maybe you'll both lose good money on the gamble before you've done."

"I think not," said Jake in his steady drawl. "I've known many a worse starter than you get home on the straight."

Saltash laughed aloud, and Toby turned with flushed cheeks and lifted eyes, alight and ardent, to her hero's face.

Saltash's glance flashed round to her, the monkeyish grin still about his mouth, and from her to Bunny who stood behind.

"No, you've never known a worse starter, Jake," he said; "and if I do get home on the straight it will be thanks to you."

Very curiously, from that moment Bunny found his brief resentment dead.

Chapter
Five

"Let's go out into the garden!" Bunny said urgently.

Dinner was over, and Maud and Saltash were at the piano at the far end of the great room. Jake and Larpent were smoking in silent companionship at a comfortable distance.

Toby, who had been very quiet the whole evening, sat slightly apart in a low chair with her hands clasped about her knees.

She lifted her eyes to him as he prowled near her, and they held a hint of mischief. At his murmured words she rose.

"You'd like to?" he questioned.

She nodded. "Of course; love it. You know the way. You lead!"

Bunny needed no second bidding. He went straight to the tall door and held it open for her. Toby, very slim and girlish in her white raiment, cocked her chin and walked out in state.

But the moment they were alone she turned upon him a face brimming with laughter.

"Oh, now we can enjoy ourselves! I've been feeling so proper all the evening. Quick! Where shall we go?"

"Into the garden," said Bunny. "Or wait! Come up on to the battlements! It's ripping up there."

She thrust her hand eagerly into his.

"I shall love that. Which way do we go?"

"Through the music-room," said Bunny.

He caught and held her hand. They ran up one of the wide stairways that branched north and south to the gallery.

Saltash's music followed them from the drawing-room as they went. He was playing a haunting Spanish love-song, and Toby shivered and quickened her pace.

Bunny opened the door and a dark passage gaped before them.

The spirit of adventure seized Bunny. He let the door swing closed and caught her hand again.

"Now we shall have some fun!" Toby said.

They went forward together for a few yards in total darkness. Then from somewhere high above them a faint light filtered through.

The steps up became narrower and more steeply spiral than before. His companion mounted so swiftly that he found it difficult to keep close to her. The ascent seemed endless.

They passed a window-slit, and Bunny suddenly awoke to the fact that the flying figure in front was trying to outdistance him. It came to him in a flash of intuition.

She was daring him, she was fooling him. Some imp of mischief had entered into her. She was luring him to pursuit, and like the whirling of a torch in a dark place, the knowledge first dazzled and then drew him.

All his pulses beat in a swift crescendo. There was a considerable mixture of Irish devilry in Bunny Brian's veins, and anything in the nature of a challenge fired him.

He uttered a wild whoop that filled the eerie place with fearful echoes, and gave chase.

It was the maddest race he had ever run. Toby fled before him like the wind, up and up, round and round the winding stair, fleet-footed, almost as though on wings, leaving him behind.

He followed, fiercely determined, putting forth his utmost strength, sometimes stumbling on the uneven stairs, yet always leaping onward, urged to wilder effort by the butterfly elusiveness of his quarry.

Once he actually had her within his reach, and then he stumbled and she was gone. He heard her maddening laughter as she fled.

The ascent seemed endless. His heart was pumping but he would not slacken. She should never triumph over him, this mocking imp, this butterfly-girl, who from the first had held him with a fascination he could not fathom.

He would make her pay for her audacity. He would teach her that he was more than a mere butt for her drollery. He would show her . . .

A door suddenly banged high above him. He realized that she had reached the top of the turret and burst out upon the ramparts.

A very curious sensation went through him. It was almost a feeling of fear. She was such a wild little creature, and her mood was at its maddest.

The chill of the place seemed to wrap him round. He felt as if icy fingers had clutched his heart.

It was all a joke, of course—only a joke! But jokes sometimes ended disastrously, and Toby, Toby was not an ordinary person. She was either a feather-brain or a genius. He did not know which.

Perhaps there was no very clear dividing line between the two. She was certainly extraordinary.

He wished he had not accepted her challenge. If he had refused to follow, she would soon have abandoned her absurd flight through the darkness.

And then suddenly he blundered into an iron-clamped door and swore again. Yes, this thing was beyond a joke.

The door resisted him and he wrestled with it furiously, as though it had been a living thing obstructing his passage.

He had begun to think that she must have bolted it on the outside when abruptly it yielded to his very forcible persuasion and he stumbled headlong into the open starlight.

He was out upon the ramparts, and dim, wooded park-lands stretched away to the sea before his dazzled eyes.

The first thing that struck him was the emptiness of the place. It seemed to catch him by the throat. There was something terrible about it.

Behind him the door clanged, and the sound seemed the only sound in all that wonderful June night. It had a fateful effect in the silence, like the tolling of a bell.

Something echoed to it in his own heart, and he knew that he was afraid.

Desperately he flung his fear aside and moved forward to the parapet. The wall was thick, but between the battlements it was only the height of his knee. Below was depth, sheer depth, stark emptiness.

He looked over and saw the stone terrace, dimly lit by the stars, far below him. The gardens were a blur of darkness out of which he vaguely discerned the glimmer of the lake among its trees.

His heart was beating suffocatingly; he struggled to subdue his panting breath. She was somewhere close to him, of course, of course. But the zest of the chase had left him. He felt dizzy, frightened, sick.

He tried to raise his voice to call her, and then realized with a start of self-ridicule that it had failed him. He leaned against the parapet and resolutely pulled himself together.

All the way back to the wall on the north side he pursued his way with fierce intention, inwardly raging, outwardly calm. He reached the obstructing wall—and found nothing.

The emptiness came all about him again. The ghostly quiet of the place clung like a tangible veil. She had evaded him again. He was powerless.

But at this point his wrath suddenly burst into flame, the hotter and the fiercer for its long restraint. He wheeled in his tracks with furious finality and abandoned his quest.

His intention was to go straight down by the way he had come and leave her to play her will-o'-the-wisp game in solitude. It would soon pall upon her, he was assured; but in any case he would no longer dance to her piping.

She had fooled him to the verge of frenzy!

Again he rounded the curve of the wall and came to the door of the turret. A great bastion of stone rose beside this, and as he reached it a small white figure darted forward from its shadow with dainty, butterfly movements, pulled at the heavy oak door and held it open with an elaborate gesture for him to pass.

It was a piece of exquisite daring, and with an older man it would have taken effect. Saltash would have laughed his quizzing, cynical laugh and accepted his defeat with royal grace.

But Bunny was young and vehement of impulse and the flame of his anger still scorched his soul with a heat intolerable. She had baffled him, astounded him, humiliated him, and his was not a nature to endure such treatment tamely.

He hung on his stride for a single moment, then hotly he turned and snatched her into his arms.

She cried out sharply as he caught her, and then she struggled and fought like a mad creature for freedom. But Bunny held her fast.

He had been hard-pressed, and now that the strain was over, all the pent passion of that long stress had escaped beyond control.

He held her, at first as a boy might hold a comrade who had provoked him to exasperation; then, as desperately she resisted him, a new element suddenly rushed like fire through his veins, and he realized burningly, overwhelmingly, that for the first time in his life he held a woman in his arms.

It came to him like a blinding revelation, and forthwith it seemed to him that he stepped into a new world. She had tried him too far, had thrown him off his balance.

He was unfit for this further and infinitely great-er provocation. His senses swam. The touch of her intoxicated him as though he had drunk a potent draught from some goblet of the gods.

He heard himself laugh passionately at her puny efforts to resist him, and the next moment she was at his mercy. He was pressing fevered kisses upon her gasping, quivering lips.

But she fought against him still. Though he kissed her, she would have none of it. She struck at him, battering him frantically with her hands, stamping wildly with her feet, till he literally swung her off the ground, holding her slender body against his breast.

"You little madcap!" he said with his hot lips against her throat. "How dare you? Do you think I'd let you go—now?"

The quick passion of his voice or the fiery pos-session of his hold arrested her. She suddenly ceased to battle with him and stiffened in his grasp as if turned to stone.

"Let me go!" she said tensely.

"I will not," said Bunny.

He was mad with the fever of youth; he held her with a fierce exultation. There could be no returning now, nor did he wish to return.

"You little wild butterfly!" he said and kissed the throbbing white throat again. "I've caught you now and you can't escape."

"You've . . . had your revenge," Toby flung back gaspingly. "You . . . you . . . you're a skunk if you take any more."

Oddly that sobered him as any protest more feminine would have failed to do. He set her on her feet, but he held her still.

"I haven't done with you," he said with a certain doggedness.

"Oh, I know that," she returned very bitterly. "You're like all the men. You can't play fair. Men don't know how."

That stung him.

"Fair or unfair, you've done all the playing so far. If you thought I was such a tame fool as to put up with it, well, that's not my fault."

"No, it's never your fault," Toby replied sharply.

She made a little vehement movement to extricate herself, but finding him obdurate abandoned the attempt.

"You're not a fool, Bunny Brian. You're a beast and a coward!"

"Be careful!" warned Bunny, his dark eyes gleaming ominously.

But she uttered a laugh of high defiance.

"Oh, I'm not afraid of you. You're not full-grown yet. You're ashamed of yourself already."

He coloured deeply at the taunt, but he maintained his hold upon her.

"All right," he said. "Say I did it all! It doesn't matter how you put it. The fact remains."

"What fact?" said Toby swiftly.

He clasped her a little closer.

"Well, do you think I'm going to let you go—after this?"

She caught her breath sharply.

"What do you mean? I . . . I . . . I don't know what you mean!"

There was quick agitation in her voice. Again she sought to free herself, and again he frustrated her. But the violence had gone out of his hold. There was even a touch of dignity about him as he replied.

"I mean, you little wild butterfly, that now I've got you, I'm going to keep you. You'll have to marry me and make the best of me."

"Marry you!" said Toby incredulously.

"Yes. What's the matter with the idea? Don't you want to?"

Bunny's good-looking young face came close to hers. He was laughing, but there was a half-coaxing note in his voice as well.

"You're mad!" Toby said tersely after a moment.

"I'm not," Bunny replied. "I'm perfectly serious. Don't you understand that when this kind of thing gets hold of you, there's no getting away from it? We can't possibly go back to where we were before, behave as if nothing had happened. You wouldn't want to, would you?"

There was a hint of pleading in his tone now. Toby made a curious little gesture that seemed to express a measure of reassurance.

"You aren't angry, are you?" Bunny asked softly.

She hesitated. "I was."

"Yes, but not now, when you've begun to realize what a jolly thing life together would be. It isn't as if we'd never met before. We're pals already."

"Yes, we're pals," said Toby, but still her voice was dubious.

"I say, be a sport!" the boy urged suddenly. "You said you weren't afraid of me. Don't chuck the best thing in life for want of a little ordinary courage!"

"What is . . . the best thing in life?" Toby asked.

His hold grew close again, but it remained gentle.

"You marry me and I'll show you!"

There was something sublime rather than ridiculous in his assurance. Toby caught her breath again as if about to laugh, and then quite suddenly, wholly unexpectedly, she began to cry.

"You poor little darling!" Bunny soothed.

She leaned her head upon his shoulder, fighting great sobs that threatened to overwhelm her. It was not often that Toby cried, and this was no mere child's distress.

Indeed there was about it something that filled her companion with a curious kind of awe. He held her closely and comfortingly, but for some reason he could not speak to her, could not even attempt to seek the cause of her trouble.

As his sister had done before him, though almost unconsciously, he sensed a barrier that he might not pass.

Toby regained her self-command at last, stood for a space in silence, her face still hidden, then abruptly raised it and uttered a little quivering laugh.

"You great big silly!" she said. "I'm not going to marry you, so there! Now let me go!"

Her tone and action put him instantly at his ease. This was the Toby he knew.

"Yes, you are going to marry me. And I shan't let you go," he said. "So there!"

She looked him straight in the face.

"No, Bunny!" she said with a little catch in

her breath. "You're a dear to think of it, but it won't do."

"Why not?" demanded Bunny.

She hesitated.

He squeezed her shoulders.

"Tell me why not!"

"I don't want to tell you."

"You've got to," he said with decision.

In the dimness his eyes looked into hers. A little shiver went through Toby.

"I don't want to," she said again.

"Go on!" commanded Bunny autocratically.

She turned suddenly and set her hands against his breast.

"Well, then, because I'm years and years older then you are . . ."

"Rot!" interjected Bunny.

"And . . . I'm not good enough for you!" finished Toby rather tremulously.

"Rats!" said Bunny.

"No, it isn't rats."

She contradicted him rather piteously.

"You've turned a silly game into deadly earnest, and you shouldn't . . . you shouldn't. I wouldn't have done it if I had known. It's such a mistake . . . it's always such a great mistake . . . to do that. You say we can't go back to where we were before, but we can . . . we can. Let's try . . . anyway!"

"We can't," said Bunny with decision. "And there's no reason why we should. Look here! You don't want to marry anyone else, do you?"

"I don't want to marry at all," said Toby.

He laughed at that.

"Darling, of course you'll marry. Come! You

might as well have me first as last. You won't get
any other fellow to suit you half as well. What?
Say you'll have me! Come, you've got to. You
don't hate me, do you?"

Again the pleading note was in his voice. She
responded to it almost involuntarily. Her hands
slipped upwards to his shoulders.

"But . . . I'm not good enough," she said again,
catching back a sob.

His arms enfolded her closely and tenderly.

"Oh, skip that! I won't listen."

"You . . . you . . . you're very silly," murmured
Toby with her head against his neck.

"No. I'm not. I'm very sensible. Look here,
we're engaged now, aren't we?" said Bunny.

"No . . . no . . . we're not!" Her voice came
muffled against his coat. "You're not to think of
such a thing for ages and ages and ages."

"Oh, rot!" he said again with impatience. "I
hate a waiting game, especially when there's nothing to wait for. You're not going to give me the
go-by now."

His face was close to her again. She put her
hand against his chin and softly pushed it away.

"Bunny!" she said.

"Well, dear?" He stood, not yielding, but suffering her check.

"Bunny!" she said again, speaking with obvious effort. "I've got to say something. You must
listen . . . just for a minute. Jake . . . Jake won't
want you to be engaged to me."

"What?" Bunny started a little, as one who suddenly remembers a thing forgotten. "Jake! What the
devil has it got to do with Jake?"

"Stop!" said Toby. "Jake's quite right. He knows. He's . . . he's older than you are. You . . . you . . . you'd better ask him."

"Ask Jake!" Bunny's wrath exploded. "I'm my own master. I can marry whom I like. What on earth should I ask Jake for?"

"You needn't if you don't want to." Toby uttered a little sigh. "But if you're wise, you will. He understands. You wouldn't. You see, I've been to a lot of different schools, Bunny, foreign ones, and I've learnt a heap of . . . other funny things.

"That's why I'm so much older than you are. That's why I don't want to get married . . . as most girls do. I never ought to marry. I know too much."

"But you'll marry me?" he said swiftly.

"I don't know," she said. "Anyway, not yet. If . . . if you can stick to me for six months . . . I . . . p'raps I'll think about it. But I think you'll come to your senses long before then, Bunny."

A desolate little note of humour sounded in her voice.

"And if you do, you'll be so glad not to have to throw me over."

"You're talking rot," said Bunny.

"No, I'm not. I'm talking sense . . . ordinary common sense. I wouldn't get engaged to any man on the strength of what happened tonight. You hadn't even thought of me in that way when we came up here."

"I'm not so sure of that." Bunny smiled. "Anyway, the mischief is done now. And you needn't be afraid I shall throw you over because . . ." an unexpected throb came into his voice, ". . . I know now. I've simply got to have you."

Toby sighed again.

"But if . . . if I'm not worth waiting for, I'm not worth having," she said.

"But why wait?" argued Bunny.

"For a hundred reasons. You're not really in love with me, for one thing." Toby spoke with conviction.

"Yes, I am." Stubbornly he contradicted her.

"No, you're not. Listen, Bunny! Love isn't just a passion-flower that blooms in a single night and then fades. You're too young really to understand, but I know . . . I know. Love is more like a vine. It takes a long while to ripen and come to perfection, and it has a lot to go through first."

Again a sense of strangeness came to Bunny. Surely this was a grown woman speaking! This was not the wild little creature he knew. But perhaps it was from perversity, her warning only served to strengthen his determination.

"You can go on arguing till midnight," he said, "you won't convince me. But look here, if you don't want anyone to know, we'll keep it to ourselves for a little while. Will that satisfy you? We'll meet and have some jolly times together in private. Will that make you any happier?"

"We shan't be engaged?" questioned Toby.

"Not if you'll kiss me without," said Bunny generously.

"Oh, I don't mind kissing you," she lifted her lips at once, "if it doesn't mean anything."

He stooped swiftly and met them with his own. His kiss was close and lingering, it held tenderness, and in a moment her arms crept round his neck and she clung to him as she returned it.

He felt a sob run through her slight frame as he

held her, though she shed no tears and made no sound, and he was stirred to a deeper chivalry than he had ever known before.

"It does mean one thing, darling," he said softly. "It means that we love each other, doesn't it?"

"It may mean that," she whispered back. "I don't know . . . very much about . . . love. No one ever . . . really . . . loved me before."

"I love you," he said. "I love you."

"Thank you," she murmured.

"You'll never run away from me again? Promise!" He held her still.

She shook her head promptly with a faint echo of the elfin laughter that had so maddened him a little earlier.

"No, I won't promise. But I'll show you where I was hiding if you like. Shall I?"

"All right. Show me!" he said.

She freed herself from him with a little spring and turned to the stone buttress against which he had found her. He followed her closely, half afraid of losing her again, but she did not attempt to elude him.

"See!" she said with a funny little chuckle. "I found this ledge."

The ledge she indicated was on a level with the parapet and not more than six inches wide. It ran square with the buttress, which on the outer side dropped sheer to the terrace.

Bunny looked and turned sick.

"You never went along there!"

She laughed again.

"Yes, I did. It's quite easy if you slide your feet. I'll show you."

"You'll do nothing of the sort!" He grabbed

her fiercely. "What in heaven's name were you thinking of? How did you learn to do these things?"

She did not answer him.

"I wanted to tease you," she said lightly. "And I did it too, didn't I? I pretended I was Andromeda when I got round the corner, but no Perseus came to save me. Only an angry dragon ramped about behind."

Bunny stared at her as if he thought her bewitched.

"But you were over by that north wall once. I'll swear you were over there."

"Oh, don't swear!" she said demurely. "It's so wrong. I wasn't there really. I only sent my voice that way to frighten you."

"Good heavens!" gasped Bunny.

She laughed again with gay *insouciance*.

"Haven't I given you a splendid evening's entertainment? Well, it's all over now, and the curtain's down. Let's go!"

She turned with her hand in his and led him back to the turret-door.

Reaching it, he sought to detain her.

"You'll never do it again? Promise, promise!"

"I won't promise anything," she said lightly.

"Ah, but you must!" he insisted. "Toby, you might have killed yourself."

Her laugh suddenly had a mocking sound.

"Oh, no! I shall never kill myself on Lord Saltash's premises."

"Why do you say that?" questioned Bunny.

"Because *que voulez-vous*? He would want me neither dead nor alive," she answered recklessly.

"A good thing too!" declared Bunny stoutly.

The echoes of Toby's laughter as she went down the chill, dark stairway had an eerie quality that sent an odd shiver through his heart.

Somehow it made him think of the unquiet spirit that was said to haunt the place, a spirit that wandered alone, always alone, in the utter desolation.

Chapter
Six

"How long is this absurd farce to go on?" Larpent asked.

"Aren't you enjoying yourself?" Saltash grinned.

Larpent looked sardonic.

Saltash took up the whisky decanter.

"My worthy buccaneer, you don't know when you're lucky. If I had a reputation like yours . . ."

He broke off, still grinning.

"Well, it's no use crying over spilt milk, is it? Let's spill some whisky instead! Say when!"

Larpent watched him, frowning.

"Thanks! That's enough. I should like an answer to my question if you've no objection. How long is this practical joke going to last?"

Saltash turned and looked upon him with a calculating eye.

"I really don't know what's troubling you. You've got everything in your favour. I'd change places with you with all the pleasure in the world if circumstances permitted."

"That isn't the point, is it?" said Larpent.

"No? What is the point?" Saltash turned again to the whisky decanter.

"Well, you've got me into a damn hole, and I want to know how you're going to get me out again." Larpent's voice was gruff and surly; he stared into his tumbler without drinking.

Saltash chuckled to himself with mischievous amusement.

"My dear chap, I can't get you out. That's just it. I want you to stay there."

Larpent muttered deeply and inarticulately and began to drink.

Saltash turned round, glass in hand, and sat down on the edge of the high cushioned fender.

"I really don't think you are greatly to be pitied. The child will soon be married and off your hands."

"Oh, that's the idea, is it?" Larpent replied. "Who's going to marry her? Young Brian?"

"Don't you approve?" said Saltash.

"I don't think it'll come off," Larpent answered with decision.

"Why not?" An odd light flickered in the younger man's eyes for an instant. "Are you going to refuse your consent?"

"I?" Larpent shrugged his shoulders. "Are you going to give yours?"

Saltash made an elaborate gesture.

"I shall bestow my blessing with both hands."

Larpent looked at him fixedly for a few seconds.

"You're a very wonderful man, My Lord," he remarked drily at length.

"Have you only just discovered that?" Saltash laughed.

"All the same, I don't believe it will come off,"
he said.

Saltash moved impatiently.

"You always were an unbeliever. But anyone
can see they were made for each other. Of course
it will come off."

"You want it to come off?" asked Larpent.

"It is my intention that it shall," said Saltash
royally.

"You're playing Providence in the girl's interest. Is that it?"

Again Larpent's eyes, shrewd and far-seeing
were fixed upon him. They held a glint of humour.

"It's a tricky job, My Lord. You'll wish you
hadn't before you've done."

"Think so?" said Saltash.

"If you haven't begun to already," said Larpent.

Saltash looked down at him with a comical
twist of the eyebrows.

"You're very analytical tonight. What's the
matter?"

"Nothing," said Larpent bluntly. "Except that
you're making a mistake."

"Indeed?" For a moment Saltash's look was
haughty; then he began to smile again. "I see you're
burning to give your advice. Fire away, if it does
you any good!"

Larpent's eyes, very steady under their fair,
bushy brows, were still unwaveringly upon him.

"No, I don't presume to give you advice. But
I'll tell you something which you may or may not
know. That young woman you have so kindly bestowed upon me as a daughter worships the ground
you tread on, and that being the case, she isn't

very likely to make a dazzling success of it if she marries young Bernard Brian."

He ceased to speak, and simultaneously Saltash jerked himself to his feet with a short French oath that sounded like the snarl of an angry animal.

He went across to the windows that were thrown wide to the summer night, and stood before one of them with his head flung back in the attitude of one who challenges the universe.

Larpent lay back in his chair with the air of a man who has said his say. He did not even glance towards his companion, and there followed a considerable pause before either of them spoke again.

Abruptly at length Saltash wheeled.

"Larpent!"

There was something of a whip-lash quality about his voice; it seemed to cut the silence.

"Why the devil do you tell me this? Can't you see that it's the very thing I'm guarding against? Young Bunny is the best remedy she could take for a disease of that kind. And, after all, she's only a child."

"Do you say that for your own benefit or for mine?" said Larpent without turning his head.

"What do you mean?" Savagely Saltash flung the question, but the man in the chair remained unmoved.

"You know quite well what I mean," he said. "You know that it isn't true."

"What isn't true?" Saltash came swiftly back across the room, moving as if goaded.

He took his tumbler from the mantelpiece and drank the contents almost at a gulp.

"Go on! May as well finish now you've begun. What isn't true?"

Larpent lounged in his chair and watched him, absolutely unmoved.

"When a thing is actually in existence, an accomplished fact, it's rather futile to talk of guarding against it," he said in his brief, unsympathetic voice.

"You've been extraordinarily generous to the imp, and it isn't surprising that she should be extraordinarily grateful. She wouldn't be human if she weren't.

"But when it comes to handing her on to another fellow, well, she may consent, but it won't be because she wants to, but because it's the only thing left. She knows well enough by this time that what she really wants is out of her reach."

Again Saltash made a fierce movement, but he did not turn or speak.

Larpent took out his pipe and began to fill it.

"You've been too good a friend to her," he went on somewhat grimly, "and you're not made of the right stuff for that sort of thing. I'm sorry for the kid because she's a bit of a pagan too, and it's hard to embrace respectability whether you want to or not."

"Oh, damn!" Saltash exclaimed suddenly and violently. "What more could any man have done? What the devil are you driving at?"

He turned upon Larpent almost menacingly and found the steady eyes, still with that icy glint of humour in them, unflinchingly awaiting his challenge.

"You want to get married," the sailor said imperturbably. "Why, in the name of all the stars of destiny, don't you marry her? She may not have blue blood in her veins, but blood isn't everything, and you've got enough for two.

"And it's my opinion you'd find her considerably easier to please than some, less strict in her views too, which is always an advantage to a man of your varying moods."

Saltash's laugh had a curious jarring sound as of something broken.

"Oh, you think that would be a suitable arrangement, do you? And how long do you think I should stick to her? How long would it be before she ran away?"

"I never speculate so far as you are concerned," said Larpent, shaking the tobacco back into his pouch with care.

"You think it wouldn't matter, perhaps?" gibed Saltash. "My royal house is so inured to scandal that no one would expect anything else?"

"I don't think she is the sort to run away," Larpent replied quietly. "And I'm pretty sure of one thing. You could hold her if you tried."

"An ideal arrangement!" sneered Saltash. "And I should then settle down to a godly, righteous, and sober life, I suppose? Is that the idea?"

"You said it," observed Larpent, pushing his pipe into his mouth.

Saltash lodged one foot on the high fender and stared at it. The sneer died out of his face and the old look, half mischievous, half melancholy, took its place.

"I haven't seriously contemplated marriage for eight years."

His mouth twitched a little as with a smile suppressed.

"Not since the day I tried to steal Maud Brian away from Jake, and failed rather signally. I don't think I've ever done anything quite so low-down since."

Larpent lighted his pipe with grave attention. "A good thing for you both that you did fail!"

"Think so?" Saltash glanced at him. "Why?"

"She isn't the woman for you."

Larpent spoke with the absolute conviction of one who knows.

"She has too many ideals. Now this sprat you caught at Valrosa has none."

"Not so sure of that," said Saltash.

"Well, no illusions anyway."

There was a hint of compassion in Larpent's voice.

"It wasn't because she trusted you that she put herself under your protection. She didn't trust you. She simply chucked herself at you with her eyes open.

"Like Jonah's whale, you were the only shelter within reach. I'd wager a substantial sum that she's never had any illusions about you. But if you held up your little finger she'd come to you. She's your property, and it isn't in her to do anything else, let her down as often as you will."

Saltash made an excruciating grimace.

"My good fellow, spare me! That's just where the shoe pinches. I've broken faith with her already. But damnation! What else could I do? I didn't choose the part of virtuous hero. It was thrust upon me.

"The gods are making sport of me. I am lost in a labyrinth of virtue and horribly, most horribly, sick of it. I nearly broke through once, but the wreck pulled me up, and when I recovered from that I was more hopelessly lost than before."

"So you are not enjoying it either!" remarked

"Look here!" he said abruptly as they drew apart from the throng. "I've got to see more of you somehow. Have you been dodging me all this time?"

"I?" said Toby.

She met his eyes with a funny little chuckle. There was spontaneous mischief in her own.

He gave her hand an admonitory squeeze.

"I'm not laughing. You're not playing the game. What's the good of my coming to the house to see you if we never meet?"

"Don't understand," said Toby briefly.

"Yes, you do. Or you can if you try. You never seem to have any liberty nowadays. Is it Maud's doing or your own?"

Toby laughed again, lightly and bafflingly.

"I can do anything I want to do."

"Oh, can you?" Bunny pounced. "Then you've got to meet me sometimes away from the rest. See? Come! That's only fair."

Toby made a face at him.

"Suppose I don't want to?"

He laughed into her eyes.

"Don't tell me that! When and where?"

She laughed back. He was hard to resist.

"I don't know. I'm too busy."

"Rot!" said Bunny.

"You're very rude," she remarked.

"I'll be ruder when I get the chance." He laughed. "Listen! I want to see you alone very badly. You're not going to let me down."

"I don't know what I'm going to do yet," said Toby.

But she could not look with severity into the handsome young face that was bent to hers. It was not in her to repulse a friendly influence. She had to respond.

"I'll tell you what you're going to do," said Bunny, marking her weakening with cheery assurance. "You'll take Chops for a walk tomorrow evening through the Burchester Woods. You know that gate by the larch copse? It's barely a mile across the down. Be there at seven, and perhaps— who knows? Perhaps Chops may meet somebody he's rather fond of."

"And again perhaps he mayn't," said Toby, suppressing a dimple.

"Oh, I say, that's shabby! You'll give him the chance anyhow?"

The pleading note sounded in Bunny's voice. Toby suddenly dropped her eyes. She looked as if she were bracing herself to refuse.

Bunny saw and quickly grappled with the danger.

"Give him the chance! You won't be sorry— afterwards."

She did not lift her eyes, but somehow the enchantment held. By a bold stroke he had entered her defences, and she could not for the moment drive him out. She was silent.

"You'll come?" whispered Bunny.

They were nearing a little group of ponies that were being held in readiness at the end of the field. Toby quickened her pace.

He kept beside her, but he did not speak again. And perhaps his silence moved her more than speech, for she gave a little impulsive turn towards him and threw him her sudden, boyish smile.

"All right. We'll come," she said.

"Hooray!" crowed Bunny softly.

"But I shan't stay long," she warned him. "And if I don't like it, I shall never come again."

"You will like it," said Bunny with confidence.

"I wonder!" said Toby with her chin in the air.

*   *   *

Bunny surpassed himself that afternoon. Wherever he went success seemed to follow, and shouts of applause reached him from all quarters.

"That young fellow is a positive genius," commented General Melrose, who had a keen eye for the game. "He ought to be in the Service. Why isn't he, Mrs. Bolton?"

"He wasn't considered strong enough," Maud said. "It was a great disappointment to him. You see, he spent the whole of his childhood on his back with spine trouble. And when that was put right he outgrew his strength."

"Ah! I remember now. You used to wheel the poor little beggar about in a long chair. Well, he's rather different now from what he was in those days. Not much the matter with him, is there?"

"Nothing now," Maud said.

"What does he do with himself?" asked the General, surveying the distant figure at that moment galloping in a far corner of the field.

"He is agent on Lord Saltash's estate at Burchester," his daughter said, suddenly entering the conversation. "He was telling me about it at luncheon. He and Lord Saltash are friends."

"Ah! To be sure!" General Melrose's look suddenly came to Maud and she felt herself colour a little.

"He is an old friend of the family," she said. "We live not far from the Castle. My husband owns the Graydown Stables."

"Oh, I know that," the General said courteously. "I know your husband, Mrs. Bolton, and I am proud to know him. What I did not know until today was that he was your husband. I never heard of your marriage."

"We have been married for eight years," she said with a smile.

"It must be at least ten since I saw you last," he said. "This girl of mine, Sheila, must have been at school in those days. You never met her?"

Maud turned to the girl.

"I don't think we have ever met before. Is this your first visit to Fairharbour?"

Sheila leaned forward. "My first visit, yes."

She was a pretty girl of twenty-two, with a quantity of soft dark hair and grey eyes that held a friendly smile.

"We don't go to the sea much in the summer as a rule. We get so much of it in the winter. Dad always winters in the South. It only seems a few weeks since we came back from Valrosa."

Maud was conscious of an abrupt jerk from Toby on her other side, and she laid a hand on her arm with the kindly intention of drawing her into the conversation.

But the next instant, feeling tension under her hand, she turned to look at her and was surprised to see that Toby was staring out across the field with wide, strained eyes.

She looked so white that Maud had a moment of sharp anxiety.

"Is anything the matter, dear?" she whispered.

An odd little tremor went through Toby. She spoke with an effort.

"I thought he was off his pony that time, didn't you?"

She kept her eyes upon Bunny, who was coming back triumphant.

"Oh, I don't think there is much danger of that." Maud smiled. "Miss Melrose was talking about Valrosa. You were there too last winter, weren't you?"

The colour mounted in Toby's face. She turned almost defiantly.

"Just for a day or two. I was at school at Geneva. I went there to join my father."

"I was at school at Geneva a few years ago," said Sheila Melrose. "You didn't go to *Mademoiselle* Denise, I suppose?"

"No," said Toby briefly. "*Madame* Beaumonde."

"I never heard of her," said Sheila. "It must have been after I left."

Toby nodded.

"I wasn't there long. I've never been anywhere long. But I've left school now, and I'm going to do as I like."

"A very wise resolution!" commented a laughing voice behind her. "It's one of the guiding principles of my life."

All the party turned, Toby with a quick exclamation muffled at birth. Saltash, attired in a white yachting suit and looking more than usually distinguished in his own fantastic fashion, stood with his hand on the back of Toby's chair.

"Quite a gathering of old friends!" he declared, smiling impartially upon all.

General Melrose stretched a welcoming hand to him.

"Hullo, Saltash! Where on earth have you sprung from? Or have you fallen straight out of the skies?"

"Like Lucifer, son of the morning!" Saltash laughed. "Well, I haven't sprung and I haven't fallen. I have simply arrived."

Toby was on her feet.

"Come and sit down!"

He shook his head.

"No, no, *ma chère*. I will stand behind you. Miss Melrose, my humble regards to you. Is the black mark still against my name?"

Sheila looked at him with a touch of hauteur that somehow melted into a smile. She had learnt her lesson at Valrosa and there was nothing to add thereto.

This man was never in earnest, and he had never intended her to think him so.

"I banned you as bold and bad long ago," she said. "I don't remember that you have done anything to change the impression."

He laughed lightly, enigmatically.

"Nothing in your presence, I fear. The Fates have always been sportive so far as I was concerned. But really I'm not such a bad sort nowadays, am I, Mrs. Bolton?"

Maud smiled upon him.

"Not so bad, I think. But please don't ask

me to be your sponsor! I really couldn't play the part."

"Ask me!" said Toby suddenly with flushed face upraised. "He saved my life when *The Night Moth* went down, when most men would only have bothered to save their own."

"What a libel!" Saltash laughed. "Don't you know I only hung on to you because you had a lifebelt on?"

"Oh, naturally!" said the General. "That would be your motive. I was sorry to hear about *The Night Moth,* but you had a lucky escape."

"I always escape somehow," remarked Saltash complacently. "*The Night Moth* wanted new engines too, that's one consolation. I've just bought another," he added, suddenly touching Toby's shoulder. "Your daddy's quite pleased with her. We've just come round from London in her."

"Oh, have you?" Eagerly Toby's eyes came up to his. "What is she like? What are you going to call her?"

"She isn't christened yet. I'm going to hold a reception on board, and Maud shall perform the ceremony. I'm calling her *The Blue Moon,* unless you can suggest something better."

Saltash's restless look went to Maud.

"I wanted to call her after you, but I was afraid Jake might object."

"I think *The Blue Moon* is much more suitable," she answered. "Is she as rare as she sounds?"

"She's rather a fine article," he answered. "You must come and see her, come and cruise in her if you will. She's only just off the slips. I was lucky to get her. She skims along like a bird."

"Why not call her *The Blue Bird?*" suggested Sheila.

He shook his head with his odd grimace.

"That is a thing I can never hope to possess, Miss Melrose. The blue moon may occur once in my life if I am exceptionally virtuous, but the blue bird never. I have ceased to hope for it."

His glance flashed beyond her.

"Young Bunny is distinguishing himself to-day. That was a fine effort."

Everyone was clapping except Toby, who sat staring before her with her hands in her lap. Her blue eyes were very wide open, but they did not seem to be watching the game.

"It will fly to you, *chérie,*" suddenly whispered a voice in her ear. "It is already upon the wing."

A little tremor went through her, but she did not turn her head. Only after a moment she slipped a hand behind her through the back of her chair.

Wiry fingers closed upon it, gripped it, let it go.

"When it comes to you, hold it fast!" came the rapid whisper. *"Il ne vient pas deux fois—l'oiseau bleu."*

Toby's lip trembled. She bit it desperately. Her look was strained. She did not attempt to speak.

"It is the gift of the gods, *chérie.*"

The words came softly at her shoulder, but they pierced her.

"We do not cast their gifts away. They come . . . too seldom."

She made a quick movement; it was almost convulsive, like the start of one suddenly awakened.

A hard breath went through her, and then she was laughing, laughing and clapping with the rest, her eyes upon the boyish, triumphant figure in front of her.

When the applause died away Saltash had departed abruptly as was his wont. And though they saw him in the distance several times, he did not return that afternoon.

Chapter
Seven

The party that gathered on the quay at Fairharbour on the hot July day when Saltash's new yacht *The Blue Moon* lay awaiting her christening was of a very gay description.

The yacht herself was decked with flags, and the hotel facing the quay, The Anchor, was also decorated with hunting. All the visitors in the town were congregated about the shore.

The yacht lay moored to the quay on which, by Saltash's orders, a long strip of red carpet had been laid leading to the gangway, which was decorated with trails of flowers.

The day was glorious and cloudless, the sea of that intense blue which melts to the horizon without any dividing line, like the blue of a smoked pearl.

Saltash's idea was to take his guests for a cruise across the bay after the ceremony, and he planned to complete the celebrations with a *fête* on the water at night.

Everything was in readiness, and by two o'clock he was already receiving his guests.

Maud and Jake stood with him, and little Eileen, very intent and serious, held Toby's hand and looked on from the background.

Captain Larpent was on the bridge, looking very forbidding, even contemptuous. He had never had any liking for the gay crowds with which it was Saltash's pleasure to surround himself.

He had the air of a magnificent Viking, above the frivolities with which he was surrounded. There was nothing of the ornamental about his rugged exterior, but his very aloofness made him imposing.

He looked straight over the heads of the buzzing throng that poured on to the deck.

General Melrose and his daughter were among the last to arrive, and with them came Bunny, very merry and handsome, his dark eyes singling out Toby in a flash as she stood with her small charge.

She had just lifted the child to stand on a ledge where she might overlook the proceedings when he joined them.

"Hullo!" he said eagerly. "I'm later than I meant to be. I've been lunching with General Melrose. Ye gods, what a crush! Where do they all come from? Well, sweetheart!" He bent to the child. "Enjoying your precious little self?"

The soft violet eyes met his with a deep contentment as she lifted her face for his kiss.

"I think it's lovely," she said earnestly.

He stood up and looked again with swift appreciation at Toby. The girl was dressed very simply in white, her vivid face shadowed by a broad straw hat. She met his look with a grimace of boyish dissatisfaction.

"Bunny! What a ghastly gathering! For goodness' sake, don't look at me like that! I feel like a painted marionette!"

"Are you painted?" Bunny asked. "You don't look it."

She made a vehement gesture of disgust.

"As soon as this show is over, I shall get into riding things and go like the . . . like the . . ."

"Like the dish when it ran away with the spoon," suggested Bunny with a grin as she paused. "Well, if you'll be the spoon I'll be the dish, and we'll show 'em all a clean pair of heels. Shall we?"

"I certainly won't be the spoon," said Toby with decision. "You can find someone else to play that part. Try Miss Melrose! She doesn't look as if she'd object."

"She's a very pretty girl," said Bunny rather aggressively.

"Of course she's a pretty girl. It's what she's for." Toby's chin went up. "She couldn't be anything else."

"Well, cheer up!" Bunny laughed. "She's not the only one on board. Do you know any of these people?"

Toby shook her head promptly.

"And don't want to! Aren't they awful? Oh, here's Jake! Wonder how much he's enjoying himself."

Whether Jake was enjoying himself or not was not apparent in his manner as he came up and shook hands with Bunny then turned to lift his little girl on to his shoulder.

"Hold tight, Innocence! What do you think of it all?"

"I think it's lovely, Daddy," she answered, clasping him closely. "Does Mummy like it too?"

He smiled at the anxiety in her question.

"Guess she'll come through it all right. She's not exactly keen on this sort of thing. But we're here, eh, Innocence? That ought to make a difference."

Old General Melrose turned sharply at the sound of the soft voice. He had not noticed Jake until that moment.

"Why, Bolton!" he said. "What are you doing here?"

Jake moved forward deliberately.

"Well, I guess I'm here in support of my wife, who has undertaken the chief part in the ceremony about to take place."

The old soldier looked at him from under beetling brows.

"Ah! Your wife! That's Maud Brian, isn't it? Somehow I always think of her as Maud Brian. So she still keeps up the old friendship with Saltash! I wonder you allow that."

Jake's red-brown eyes held a smile.

"She pleases herself, Sir, and she pleases me."

"That a child of yours?" asked the General abruptly. "But I needn't ask. She's got Maud's eyes. Sheila, come and see this kiddie of Maud's!"

He spoke imperiously over his shoulder, and Sheila turned in answer. Her soft eyes kindled.

"Oh, what a darling! How do you do, Mr. Bolton? I know you well by name. And this is your little girl? What is her name?"

"Eileen," whispered the child, clinging rather nervously to Jake's shoulder.

"Innocence!" said Jake.

"Ah! How sweet!" the girl said. "I must get your mummy to bring you to see me. Would you like to, I wonder?"

"I think so," said Eileen shyly.

"Maybe you'll come and see her first," said Jake. "I should like you to see the stud, Sir. We've got some stock that I think would interest you."

"That would be delightful," Sheila said in her gracious way. "We are here for another fortnight. I had no idea it was such a lovely place."

"Have you seen Burchester?" asked Bunny. She turned to him.

"Never. I want to see it. Lord Saltash said something about it the other day, so I am hoping there is a chance of doing so. You are very fond of it, Sir Bernard?"

"Yes. It's my job just now. I'm head keeper." Bunny laughed. "Miss Larpent thinks I'm very inefficient, but I do my best."

"I never said so," said Toby.

She flushed at his obvious intention of drawing her into the group, but Sheila Melrose at once held out a welcoming hand.

"Miss Larpent, do you know I can't help feeling that I've seen you somewhere before? Yet I can't quite remember where. Could it have been at Valrosa?"

"Oh, no!" said Toby. "It couldn't possibly have been there."

"And yet I can't help thinking it must have been," said Sheila, looking at her with knitted brows. "Were you at that fancy-dress affair at the

Casino Hotel? I have a feeling I have seen you somewhere in fancy dress."

"Never!" said Toby with decision. "You must be thinking of someone else."

Sheila still looked at her with puzzled eyes.

"Wait! I shall remember in a moment. It was someone exactly like you, I know, someone dressed as a boy."

Toby made a sudden sharp movement and clapped her hands excitedly.

"Look! Look! There goes the bottle! I hope she'll manage to break it!"

Sheila's attention was instantly diverted. The crowd surged forward. Maud, with Saltash on her right and Larpent on her left, stood by the rail. She held up a bottle that gleamed golden in the sun.

Saltash was laughing. He stood bare-headed, his dark face alight. Toby's eyes went to him in a single flashing glance and remained fixed.

Bunny, looking at her, was for the moment curiously moved. It was as if he looked from afar upon some sacred fire that had suddenly sprung into ardent flame before a distant shrine.

Then came Maud's voice, sweet and clear, speaking the name of the yacht, and like a golden flame the bottle curved through the pearllike ether and crashed upon the bows.

A murmur went up and then a shout. The bottle had broken, and the wine rushed in a sparkling cascade to the water.

Something impelled Bunny. He gripped Toby by the elbow. He almost shook her.

"Hooray!" he yelled. "It's done! She's off!"

Toby looked at him with the eyes of a dreamer, eyes in which a latent fear underlay the reverence. Then, meeting his eyes, she seemed to awake.

Her features contracted for a moment, but she controlled them swiftly and laughed. Laughing, she drew him away.

The yacht had throbbed into movement. The ropes were being flung aboard. They were steaming away, and a great blast went up from the siren as they drew from the quay.

Everywhere was tumult, rejoicing. People were shouting, talking, laughing, waving hats and handkerchiefs. The whole world seemed a buzz of merriment, and out of the very thick of it, Toby's voice, small and tense, spoke into Bunny's ear.

"Let's get away! Let's go to Lord Saltash and ... and ... and congratulate."

Her hand was on his arm. She pulled at it urgently, insistently. And Bunny went with her, moved again, he knew not where, by that feeling that something had frightened her.

He grasped her hand and made a way for her through the crowd. They went to the laughing group in the bows. Saltash was standing close to Maud. He was making some careless jest to her when suddenly he turned and found the boy and girl hand in hand behind him.

His swift look flashed over them, and then in his sudden way he put a hand on the shoulder of each. It was a lightning touch, and he laughed oddly as he did it, as a man laughs who covers some hidden hurt.

"We came to congratulate," said Bunny. "Good luck to her."

And Saltash, with his royal air of graciousness, replied lightly.

"I thank you for your congratulations, my children; but may the luck be yours! I see it coming."

And with that he moved away among his guests, leaving a trail of merriment wherever he went, save where the boy and girl stood together in the bows in a silence that neither seemed able to break.

* * *

That night Fairharbour Bay looked like a velvet bed on which glittered many jewels. *The Blue Moon*, lighted from bows to stern, lay in the centre, and from her deck there went up showers of coloured rockets that fell like burning rain upon the sea.

There was a string band on board, and the strains floated across the water as echoes from another world, a wonder-world of soft melodies and laughing voices and lightly splashing oars.

Toby sat in the stern of a boat with a single rower in front of her, and trailed her fingers through the magic water. She was bare-headed, and the breeze of the summer night stirred tenderly the golden ringlets that clustered about her brow.

Her face, seen now and then in the flare of the rockets, had a strange look, almost a look of dread. Her blue eyes were very wide open, like the eyes of a startled child.

She spoke scarcely at all, and Bunny did not urge her. Only, as he rowed, he watched her with grave determination on his boyish face.

He had claimed her as his partner early in the evening, and she had made no attempt to thwart him; but something in that half-scared silence of hers moved him very deeply. His own was protective, resolutely reassuring.

Once, when she started nervously at an unexpectedly loud report from one of the rockets, he spoke to her as he would have spoken to a small, frightened animal.

"It's all right. I'll pull out a bit, shall I? These things make such a beastly row."

She thanked him in an undertone, and he began to row steadily away from the yacht and the thronging boats.

"You tell me when I've gone far enough," he said.

But she did not tell him, and he rowed on and on through the dark water, with only the rhythmic splashing of the oars to fill the silence between them.

They left the laughter and the noises behind and began to draw towards the far corner of the bay. The shore rose steeply from the water here, and there came to them the soft breaking of the waves against the cliff as they neared it.

Toby came out of her silence with a jerk.

"Bunny, do you really think it would answer?"

"Sure!" said Bunny promptly.

He drew in his oars with the words, and they drifted on the summer tide.

Toby was looking at him in the starlight with a dumb and piteous irresolution in her eyes.

Bunny leaned to her as he sat, with outstretched hands.

"You poor little frightened mouse! What is it that's troubling you? Do you think I wouldn't make you happy?"

"I think you'd try," she said dubiously.

For a few seconds she hung back, hesitating; then swiftly, almost with the gesture of one who casts aside a burden, she threw out her trembling hands and thrust them into his.

He took them and held them fast, drawing them gently to him till he had them against his heart.

"I would try, sweetheart," he said softly.

"Would you?" whispered Toby. "Would you?"

She went nearer to him; he could feel her trembling from head to foot.

"You think I wouldn't succeed?" he asked her tenderly. "You think I'd make you sorry?"

"I don't know," she answered quiveringly. "I . . . I'm thinking most of you."

"Wondering whether it would be good for me to have my heart's desire?" jested Bunny softly. "Think it would be too much for me, my darling?"

"No . . . no!" said Toby. "Not that! Only wondering if you are wanting the right thing . . . wondering if the thing you call your heart's desire will bring you happiness. It . . . it doesn't always, you know, Bunny. Life is like that."

Her voice sank a little.

"What do you know about life?" he said.

She shook her head, her face downcast.

"Oh, too much, too much!"

Bunny sat motionless for a moment or two, but his hold was strong and comforting. At length, very gently he began to draw her nearer.

He almost expected her to resist him, but she did not. As he drew her she yielded, till with a sob she suffered herself to be drawn close into his arms.

He had her on the seat beside him, her face hidden against his shoulder. He laid his cheek down upon her hair and sat silent.

Toby was sobbing a little and he patted her shoulder soothingly, but he did not speak until, with a quivering sigh, she relaxed against him and was still.

"Toby, Mavourneen," he said in a whisper, "I'm going to tell you something that's come to me lately, something I've guessed. You needn't answer me. I don't want you to answer me, only to know that I know.

"There's another man in your heart, and he's got a bigger place than I have—at present. No, don't tremble, darling! It's all right. I know, I know. He's the sort that women simply can't keep out. He's a fine chap too, and I'm fond of him, always have been.

"But, look here, Mavourneen, you're not going to break your precious little heart over him; you know quite well it's no use, don't you? You know—well, anyhow to a certain extent—you know what he is, don't you?"

He paused for an answer, but Toby quivered in his arms and was silent.

He put up a hand and pressed her head closer to his breast.

"He'll never marry. He doesn't mean to. He almost told me so the other day. But Toby, he takes a friendly interest in you and me. He'd like us to have each other. Don't you think . . ."

His voice had a hint of humour.

"Don't you think we might fix it up just to

please him? P'raps some day we may find that we've pleased ourselves as well."

"Oh, my dear!" Toby whispered.

Her arm crept round his neck, but she did not lift her head. He clasped her more closely and went on very softly.

"I love you enough to think of your happiness first, my darling. You're not happy now. I know that all right. But you will be, I swear you shall be, if you will marry me. You like me just a bit, don't you? And you wouldn't be afraid to trust yourself to me?"

"No," murmured Toby with an effort. "I wouldn't be . . . afraid."

"Then you'll give me my chance?" he urged gently. "You'll put your dear little hand into mine and trust me? Will you, darling? Will you?"

But Toby was silent.

"Won't you?" he said in a whisper.

Her arm tightened about his neck. She was breathing quickly, nervously. From across the water came the sounds of laughter and cheering, the softened strains of the band that played on the deck of *The Blue Moon.*

Close at hand was only the low wash of the waves as they lapped against the cliff. They floated quite alone over the dark depths, rising and falling with the slow heave of the tide, but making no headway.

"Won't you?" Bunny said again after a long silence.

And suddenly Toby raised her head and spoke.

"I will do . . . whatever you wish."

There was a slight break in her voice, but it held no indecision. Her eyes looked straight into his in the starlight. He saw them shining and knew that they were big with tears.

But she did not flinch from his look, or start as his lips came to hers. She slipped her other arm about his neck and clasped him close.

"You'll be good to me, Bunny?" she said in a whisper.

And he answered her deeply, his lips against her own.

"I will be good to you, my darling, so help me, God!"

Chapter
Eight

Saltash came no more during the summer days. He had departed in his abrupt way for his first pleasure cruise in *The Blue Moon,* taking no friend, save the ever-present Larpent, to relieve the monotony.

No one knew where they were bound, or if the voyage was to be long or short. He dropped out of his circle as a monkey drops from a tree, and beyond a passing wonder at his movements no one questioned either motive or intention.

Meanwhile the summer crowds came and went at Fairharbour. The Anchor Hotel was crowded with visitors, and Sheila and her father began to talk of departure for Scotland.

Jake had gone to an important race-meeting in the North, and it seemed that Bunny's suggestion to show them the stud had been forgotten.

But on an afternoon in late August, after a hotly contested polo-match, as he stood with a fizzing drink in his hand talking to Sheila, she abruptly reminded him of it.

"It's quite a fortnight since you promised to show me the horses," she said.

He started.

"Is it? I'm awfully sorry. I hadn't forgotten, but somehow I've had a lot to think about lately. You must come and have tea with Maud. When will you come?"

Sheila laughed a little.

"Hadn't you better ask Maud?"

"Good gracious, no!" said Bunny. "That'll be all right. She and Toby are always at home just now, and of course she will be pleased to see you any time. When can you come?"

"Well, we are leaving the day after tomorrow," Sheila answered.

"Tomorrow, then!" said Bunny promptly.

"Your sister may not want us at such short notice," she said, hesitating.

"Oh, rubbish!" said Bunny with a grin. "Of course she will! Have you seen the Castle yet?"

"Yes. We lunched there with Lord Saltash before he left. It's a horribly grim place. I didn't like it much."

"It's a magnificent place!" said Bunny stoutly. "It's completely thrown away on Charlie, of course, but I love every stone of it."

"What a pity it doesn't belong to you!" commented Sheila. "I wonder where you will live when you are married."

Bunny flushed a little.

"We're not marrying at present, but I'm hoping to stick to my job when we do."

"Oh, are you? Does Miss Larpent like that idea?" Faint surprise sounded in Sheila's tone.

"I don't know why she shouldn't," said Bunny, quick to detect it. "She's keen on the country, keen on riding, and so on. She'd hate to live in town."

"Would she?" said Sheila with a hint of incredulity.

Bunny turned on her.

"Why do you say that? She's very young, hardly more than a kid. She doesn't care for people and towns. Why should she?"

He put the question almost indignantly, and Sheila smiled at him pacifically.

"I don't know in the least why she should. I only had a sort of idea that she might. She is very pretty, isn't she? And pretty girls don't generally care to be buried before they have had their fling . . . not always then."

"Oh, you think she doesn't get any fun!" said Bunny, still somewhat resentful.

"No . . . no, of course I don't! You know best what she likes. I only wonder that Maud didn't think of giving her just one season in town. It would be rather good for her, don't you think?"

"I don't know," said Bunny rather shortly. "Maud isn't keen on town. I think she's better where she is."

"You're afraid she'd slip through your fingers if she saw too much of the world?" Sheila laughed.

"No, I'm not!" declared Bunny, frowning. "I hadn't thought about it. But I'd hate her to get old and sophisticated. Her great charm is in being —just what she is."

"Oh, she has plenty of charm," Sheila admitted, and her own brows drew a little in thought. "I wish I could remember who it is she reminds me of. That is the worst of having such a large circle."

"She isn't like anyone I've ever met," declared Bunny and gulped down his drink abruptly. "Well, I must be going. You'll come up tomorrow, then, you and the General. I shall be there, and I'll tell Maud you're coming."

"You are sure we had better come?" Sheila said.

"Of course! Maud will be delighted. I'm sorry you weren't asked before. About three, then— if that suits you! Good-bye!"

He smiled his pleasant, boyish smile and departed.

But as he raced back from Fairharbour in his little two-seater car to meet his young *fiancée* on the down, the memory of Sheila's words came back to him and he frowned again.

It was true that they were not thinking of marriage for the next few months, and their plans were still somewhat vague, but the idea of waiting while Toby had her fling for a whole season in London revolted him.

He could not have said definitely why, save that he wanted to keep her just as she was in his eyes, fresh and young and innocent. He was angry with Sheila for having suggested it, and he wanted to thrust the matter from his mind.

Yet when he found himself alone with Toby, walking along the brow of the furze-strewn down, he attacked the subject with characteristic directness.

"Sheila Melrose thinks you ought to have a season in town before we get married. Would you like to do that?"

Toby looked up at him with her clear eyes wide with surprise.

"What the blazes has it to do with Sheila Melrose?"

"Nothing, of course." He laughed briefly. "Less than nothing. It's just a point of view. She thinks you're too pretty to be buried before you've had your fling—rot of that sort."

"My fling!" said Toby, and with a sudden gesture that was almost of shrinking drew his arm more closely round her shoulders. "I should loathe it and you know it."

He held her to him.

"Of course you would. I should myself. I hate the smart set. But you know you are awfully pretty, and I don't want to do anything unfair."

"Rubbish!" Toby exclaimed.

He bent his face to hers.

"Are you beginning to care for me—just a little—by any chance?"

She laughed and flushed, twining her fingers in his without replying.

Bunny pursued his point.

"You'd sooner marry me out of hand than go hunting London for someone more to your liking, would you?"

"Oh, much!" said Toby. "But you see I hate London."

"And you don't hate me?" persisted Bunny, his dark eyes very persuasive.

She dropped her own before them and was silent.

"Say it, sweetheart!" he urged.

She shook her head.

"Let's talk about something else!"

"All right," said Bunny boldly. "Let's talk of getting married! It's high time we began."

"Oh, I didn't mean that!" Toby answered quickly.

He laughed at her softly.

"Of course you didn't! But you were thinking about it all the same. Do you know old Bishop is going to clear out and go and live in Fairharbour? I shall be left alone then. It's rather beastly living alone you know, darling."

"You haven't tried it yet," said Toby.

"No. But I know what it'll feel like. I shall hate it."

Bunny spoke with gloomy conviction.

Toby suddenly laughed.

"No one to grouse to! It would be rather dull, certainly. Why didn't you fall in love with Sheila Melrose?"

"Sheila Melrose! Why on earth should I?" Bunny spoke with some sharpness.

Toby lifted mischievous eyes.

"She's pretty and graceful and accomplished. She'd make a charming Lady Brian, and she has an estate of her own for you to manage. It . . . it would be . . . a highly suitable arrangement for you both."

"Don't talk rot!" broke in Bunny with sudden heat.

His hold tightened upon her, and she made a quick, instinctive movement as though to free herself.

"I'm not! You know I'm not! You know quite well that if . . . if . . . if it hadn't been for me . . . because you chanced to meet me first . . . you certainly would have . . . have fallen in love with her!"

Toby spoke breathlessly, stammering a little.

Her face was averted and she was trying very hard
to resist the closer drawing of his arms.

But there were times when Bunny would
not endure resistance, and this was one of them.
He simply ignored it, till abruptly she yielded to
his mastery.

And then in a moment he was tender again.

"Why did you say that?" he said, bending low
to look into her downcast face. "Tell me why you
said it! Are you jealous by any chance?"

"Oh, no!" declared Toby with vehemence.
"No! No! No!"

"Then why?" he persisted.

Then with sudden intuition:

"You don't like her, do you?"

Toby's face was burning.

"It . . . it's she that doesn't like me."

"Oh, that's a mistake," said Bunny decidedly.
"Everyone likes you."

She shook her head.

"She doesn't. She thinks I'm bad form, and
I daresay she's right. She also thinks . . ."

She lifted her face suddenly, challenging him.
him.

"She also thinks that I set out to catch you
. . . and succeeded."

"She doesn't!" declared Bunny. "That's rot,
damn rot! You are not to say it. She's a very
nice girl and ready to be friendly with you if you'll
let her."

Toby made a rude face.

"I knew you were getting fond of her! She's
pretty and stylish, much more in your line than
I am. Why don't you go and ask her to marry you?
She wouldn't say 'No'."

She flung the words with a little quivering laugh. She was trembling in his hold.

Bunny's eyes had flashed to sudden anger. He had taken her by the shoulders almost as if he would shake her.

"Toby, be quiet!" he commanded. "Do you hear? You're going too far! What do you mean by talking in this strain? What has she done to you?"

"Nothing!" gasped back Toby, backing away from him in a vain effort to escape. "She hardly knows me even. It's just instinct with her and she can't help it. But she likes you well enough not to want you to marry me. You don't suppose ... you don't suppose ..."

The words came breathlessly, jerkily.

"You ... you really don't suppose, do you, that ... that she made that suggestion about a season in town for my sake?"

"What other reason could she have had?" demanded Bunny sternly.

Toby was laughing, but her laughter had a desperate sound.

"How green you are! Must I really tell you that?"

"Yes. Go on! Tell me!"

His voice was hard. Hard also was the grip of his hands. He knew that in the moment he released her she would turn and flee like a fleeing hare.

There was fear in the blue eyes that looked up to his, but they held a glare of defiance as well. Her small white teeth showed clenched between her laughing lips.

"Go on! Tell me!" he reiterated. "You shan't go, I swear—until you tell me."

"Think I'm . . . think I'm afraid of you?" challenged Toby with boyish bravado.

"I think you'll answer me," he said, and abruptly his tone fell level, dead level.

He looked her straight in the eyes without anger, without mercy.

"And you'll answer me now too. What other reason could Miss Melrose have for making that suggestion if it was not intended for your benefit? Now answer me!"

His face was pale, but he was master of himself. Perhaps he had learned from Jake that fundamental lesson that those who would control others must first control themselves.

He still held her before him, but there was no violence in his hold. Neither was there any tenderness. It was rather of a judicial nature.

And oddly at that moment a sudden gleam of appreciation shot up in Toby's eyes. She stood up very straight and faced him, unflinching.

"I don't mind answering you," she said. "Why should I? Someone will tell you sooner or later if I don't. She said that because she knew, and she wanted you to know, that I am not the sort of girl that men want to . . . marry."

She was quite white as she spoke the words, but she maintained her tense erectness. Her eyes never stirred from his.

Bunny stood motionless, staring at her. He looked as if he had been struck a blinding blow.

"What on earth do you mean?" he asked slowly at last.

The tension went out of Toby. She broke into her funny little laugh.

"Oh, I won't tell you any more! I won't! She

thinks I'm too attractive, that's all. I can't imagine why, can you? You never found me so, did you, Bunny?"

The old provocative sweetness flashed back into her face. She went within the circle of his arms with a quick nestling movement, as of a small animal that takes refuge after strenuous flight.

She was still panting a little as she leaned against him.

And Bunny relaxed, conscious of a vast relief that outweighed every other consideration.

"You monkey! You're playing with me! How dare you torment me like this? You shall pay for it to the last least farthing. I will never have any mercy on you again."

He kissed her with all the renewed extravagance of love momentarily denied, and the colour flooded back into Toby's face as the dread receded from her heart.

She gave him more that day than she had ever given him before, and in the rapture of possession he forgot the ordeal that she had made him face.

Only later did he remember it, her strange reticence, her odd stumbling words of warning, her curious attitude of self-defence. And he felt as if, in spite of his utmost resolution, she had somehow succeeded in baffling him after all.

It was late that evening that Bunny strolled alone to smoke a reminiscent pipe along his favourite glade of larches in Burchester Park. He had had his way with Toby. She had promised to marry him as soon as old Bishop's retirement left the house in the hollow at his disposal.

But somehow, though he had gained his end, he was not conscious of elation. Sheila Melrose's words had disturbed him no less than Toby's own peculiar interpretation of them.

There was a very strong instinct of fair play in Bunny Brian, and now that he had won his point, he was assailed by a grave doubt as to whether he were acting fairly towards the girl. She was young, but then many girls married young.

It was not really her youth that mattered; neither, when he came to sift the matter, was it the fact that she had had so little opportunity of seeing the world.

But it was something in Toby's eyes, something in Sheila's manner, that gave him pause. He asked himself, scarcely knowing why, if it would not be fairer after all to wait.

He removed his pipe from his mouth and looked around him.

"Hullo!" said a voice he knew. "Do I intrude?"

Saltash stepped suddenly out of the shadow of the larches and met him with outstretched hand.

"Hullo!" said Bunny with a start.

A quick smile of welcome lighted his face, and Saltash's eyes flashed in answer. He gripped the boy's hand with fingers that closed like springs.

"What are you doing here?" he enquired.

"Just what I was going to ask you," replied Bunny. "I often come here in the evening. It's my favourite look-out. But you . . ."

"I do the same for the same reason," said Saltash.

"I thought you were far away on the high seas," said Bunny.

"Well, I was." Saltash laughed. "But I don't stay there, my good Bunny. *The Blue Moon* developed engine trouble, nothing very serious, but we brought her back to recuperate. You can never tell what you may be in for on a first voyage. Also I was curious to see how affairs here were progressing. How goes it, *mon ami?* Is all well?"

"Well enough," said Bunny.

Saltash linked a friendly hand in his arm.

"Have you and Nonette settled when to get married yet?"

Bunny stiffened momentarily, as if his instinct were to resent the kindly enquiry. But the next instant he relaxed again with impulsive confidence.

"Well, it is more or less settled. But I'm wondering, you know, Charlie, she's rather young to be married, isn't she? She hasn't seen much of the world so far. You don't think it's shabby, do you, to marry her before she's had the same sort of chances as other girls?"

"Good heavens, no!" said Saltash.

He gave Bunny an odd look from under brows that were slightly twisted.

"What made you think of that?"

Bunny's face was red. He leaned his arms on the gate and looked out across the valley.

"Sheila Melrose put it to me this afternoon, though I must admit it had crossed my mind before. She hasn't met many people, you know, Charlie. And as I said, she's young. I don't want to take an unfair advantage."

"Life is too short to think of these things," said Saltash abruptly. "Marry her while you can get her, and don't be an ass about it! If I had done the same thing in my youth, I should have been better off than I am at present."

Bunny smiled a little.

"You would probably have been wishing you'd done the other thing by this time."

"Much you know about it!" returned Saltash with a whimsical frown. "Now look here! What I've really come back for is to see you married. All this preliminary messing about is nothing but a weariness to the flesh. Get it over, man! There's nothing on earth to wait for. Larpent's willing enough. In fact, he agrees with me, the sooner the better."

"He would!" said Bunny with a touch of bitterness.

"Well, you can't ask for anything better," maintained Saltash. "He's got his job, and he's not what you could call a family man. He's not a waster either, so you needn't put on any damned airs, *mon vieux*."

"I didn't!" said Bunny hotly.

Saltash laughed and clapped a hand on his shoulder.

"Look here! I'm talking for the good of your soul. Don't take any more advice, certainly not Sheila Melrose's! You go straight ahead and marry her! You've got money, I know, but I hope you won't chuck your job on that account. Stick to it, and you shall have the Dower House to live in while I yet cumber the ground, and Burchester Castle as soon as I'm under it!"

"What?" said Bunny.

He turned almost fiercely.

"Charlie! Stop it! You're talking rot. You always do. I don't want your beastly Castle. You've got to marry and get an heir of your own. I'm damned if I'm going to be adopted by you!"

Saltash was laughing carelessly, mockingly, yet there was about him at the moment a certain royal self-assurance that made itself felt.

"You'll do as you're told, *mon ami*. And you'll take what the gods send without any cavilling. As for me, I go my own way. I shall never marry. I shall never have an heir of my own blood. Burchester means more to you than it does to me. Therefore Burchester will pass to you at my death. Think you and Toby will be happy here?"

"Damn it!" said Bunny, still fiercely disconcerted. "You talk as if you were going to die tomorrow."

"Oh, probably not," said Saltash airily. "But I doubt if I live to a rakish old age. I'm a man that likes taking chances, and those who dice with the high gods are bound to throw a blank some day."

For a moment the mockery died down in his eyes and he looked more nearly serious than Bunny had ever seen him. He patted the shoulder under his hand.

"Life is rather a rotten old show when you've tried everything and come to the end. And you know for a damn certainty that you'll never taste any good fruit again. But you will never know what that feels like, *mon ami*. You've had the sense to play a straight game, and you'll find it pays in the long run.

"Jake taught you that, eh? You may thank your own particular lucky star that you had him for a brother-in-law instead of me."

"Don't talk rot!" said Bunny gruffly.

Saltash stretched up his arms with a laugh.

"No, we'll talk sense, good square sense. I take it you'll continue to manage the estate for the present? If you get bored, we'll find an agent, but I'm satisfied with things as they are.

"We'll go round and have a look at the old Dower House tomorrow. It has a fairly decent position, you know—overlooks Graydown. That ought to please you both."

Bunny turned upon him.

"Oh, confound it, Charlie! I can't talk about this. I couldn't possibly take it. You're too damned generous. I've never done anything to deserve it."

"Oh, yes, you have!" said Saltash unexpectedly. "You've done a good many things for me. You have always been the *bon ami* whatever I did, from your childhood upwards."

His dark face laughed with friendly warmth into the boy's troubled eyes.

"Always stuck up for me, haven't you, Bunny?"

"Oh, but that's rot!" objected Bunny. "A man is bound to stick up for his pals."

"Even though he knows they're not worth it?" Saltash laughed. "Yes, that's just what I like about you. It's the one point on which we touch. But I'm not sure that even you would stick up for me if you knew precisely what sort of rotter you were sticking up for."

"Oh, shut up!" replied Bunny.

"Bien, mon cher! We return to your affairs. Have you put up the banns yet? I presume you will allow me to be best man? Get it over soon, I beseech you! I can't stay here indefinitely. As a matter of fact, I'm due in Scotland at the present moment. Can't you fix it up immediately?

"And you can have the little car and leave of absence till you've got over it. Old Bishop can run this show till the winter. Maud can fit up the Dower House for you. And I shall feel at liberty to roam the desert once more—unencumbered."

"You're jolly decent to me!" said Bunny.

"Think so?" Saltash's brows twitched humourously. "I seem to be developing a taste for worthy deeds. But there's no reason on earth why you two shouldn't get married and done for as soon as possible. I'll see Larpent tonight and tell him, and you can go and see the parson about it tomorrow.

"You'll find Nonette won't put any obstacles in the way. She's a good child and does as she's told."

"No, Toby won't mind," Bunny said, a sudden memory of her quick surrender flooding his soul. "By Jove, Charlie! You are a good sort to help me like this. There's no one else that can get things moving as you can."

"Oh, you can count on me for that." Saltash laughed. "I never was a drifter. Life is too short. We'll meet again tomorrow, then. Come and dine if you like, and tell me what you've arranged! Good night!"

He turned in his sudden fashion.

"Good luck to you!"

He was gone upon the words, vanishing into the larches almost noiselessly as he had come, and Bunny was left alone.

He stood motionless at the gate for some time longer, gazing out over the quiet, night-wrapt down. There was no elation in his attitude, only a deep thoughtfulness.

He had never understood Charlie, though oddly enough he had always believed in him. But tonight for the first time a curious doubt pierced his mind, a doubt that recurred again and again, banishing all sense of exultation.

Why had Charlie returned like this? Why was he so eager to meddle in this affair? Why so recklessly generous? He had a strong feeling that there was something behind it all, some motive unrealized, some spur goading him, of which he, Bunny, might not approve if he came to know of it.

He wished he could fathom the matter. It was unlike Saltash to take so much trouble over anything. He felt as if in some inexplicable fashion he were being tricked.

He put the thought from him, but he could not drive it away. Just as he had felt himself baffled a little earlier by Toby, so now he felt the same inability to comprehend Saltash.

He seemed to be groping at a locked door, feeling and feeling for a key that always eluded him.

He turned homewards at length, dissatisfied and ill at ease, yet calling himself a fool for scenting a mystery that did not exist.

* * *

The Graydown Stables were always a model of well-ordered efficiency, and it had ever been Bunny's pride to show them to his friends. But he awaited General Melrose and his daughter on the following afternoon in a mood of some impatience.

He had arrived early in the hope of finding Toby, but his young *fiancée* was nowhere to be found. She had gone out riding, Maud said, immediately after luncheon, and he realized with some disgust that he had forgotten to tell her on the previous day of his coming.

"She will be in to tea, dear," Maud said, and he was obliged to content himself with the prospect of seeing her and acquainting her with Saltash's energetic interest on their behalf after the visitors had gone.

He had an urgent desire for Toby that afternoon, and he was inclined somewhat unreasonably to resent her absence. But when at length the hoot of the General's car warned him of his visitors' advent, as they turned in at the gate, he was suddenly conscious of a feeling of relief that he was alone.

Toby was not at ease with them. She fancied they disapproved of her, and whether the fancy was justified or not he was glad that she was not there to meet him. He determined to get the business over as quickly as possible.

The time passed with astonishing rapidity, and the chiming of the great stable-clock awoke Bunny at length to the fact that the afternoon was practically over.

"Maud will think we are never going in to tea," he said with a laugh, turning back from the gate into the training-field, where they had been inspecting some of the colts. "You'll come round to the house, won't you? She is expecting you, said I was to be sure to bring you in."

Sheila smiled and accepted the invitation.

"We were hoping to see Mrs. Bolton to say good-bye. Is Miss Larpent not here today?"

"Yes, she's out riding," Bunny said. "She may be in any moment. It's a pity Jake is away. He is expected back some time next week."

"Yes, I'm sorry to have missed him," said the General. "Tell him that I've enjoyed seeing the animals and I think he has a very fine show!"

"Why," Bunny exclaimed suddenly. "Hullo! There is Saltash! And Toby!"

Two figures had come suddenly round the corner of some stables, walking side by side. Both were in riding-dress, but the day being hot, the girl had discarded her long coat and was carrying it without ceremony over her arm.

Her silk shirt was open at the neck, her soft hat pushed jauntily down on the side of her head. She was laughing as she came, and she looked like a merry little cowboy straight from the prairies.

The man who moved beside her was laughing also. There was no grace about him, only that strange, unstudied kingliness that had earned for him the title of "Rex."

He was swift to see the advancing visitors, and swept the hat from his head with a royal gesture of greeting.

Toby's face flushed deeply; she looked for the moment inclined to run away. Then with an impulse half defiant, she restrained herself and caught back the smile that had so nearly vanished.

She slapped the switch against her gaitered leg with boyish swagger and advanced.

A quick frown drew Bunny's forehead as he observed her attitude. He spoke impetuously, almost before they met.

"You look like a girl out of a comic opera. Why don't you put your coat on?"

Toby made a face at him.

"Because it's cooler off. You can carry it if you like."

She threw it to him nonchalantly with the words and turned forthwith to Sheila.

"Have you just been round the Stables? Grilling, isn't it? I've been exercising one of the youngsters. He nearly pulled my arms out. We've been practising some jumps."

"Then you shouldn't," put in Bunny. "The ground's too hard for jumping."

Toby turned upon him with a flash of temper.

"No one asked for your opinion. I know a safe jump when I see one. Are you coming in to tea, Miss Melrose? I should think you're wanting it. Yes? What's the matter?"

She flung the two questions in a different tone, sharply, as though startled. Sheila was looking at her oddly, very intently, a species of puzzled recognition in her eyes.

Toby backed away from her, half laughing, yet with something that was not laughter on her face.

"What can be the matter? Is it . . . is it my riding breeches? Here, Bunny! Let me have my coat!"

She turned swiftly with extended arms.

"Quick! Before Miss Melrose faints! I've given her the shock of her life."

"No! No!" protested Sheila, recovering. "Don't be absurd! You reminded me so vividly of someone, that's all. I don't quite know who, even yet."

Bunny helped Toby into the coat without a word. There was grim displeasure on his face. The General and Saltash were talking together, and for the moment the three stood there alone.

Toby turned round laughing.

"How ridiculous you are!" she said to Bunny. "You've seen me in this get-up heaps of times before, and will again. Miss Melrose, I forgot you hadn't. I'm horribly sorry to have shocked you. Shall we go in for tea now?"

The puzzled look was still in Sheila's eyes, though she smiled in answer.

"I am not shocked ... of course. But ... but ..."

"Yes?" said Toby.

She spoke in the same brief, staccato note; the word was like a challenge. Saltash turned suddenly round.

"I have just been complimenting Miss Larpent on the excellence of her get-up," he said lightly. "We met at the gate on the down, and I have been witnessing some very pretty horsemanship. Miss Melrose, I hear you are leaving tomorrow, and am quite desolated in consequence. It is always my luck to be left behind."

The hard little smile that only he could ever provoke was on Sheila's lips as she turned to him.

"For such a rapid rider, you are indeed unfortunate."

He laughed with careless effrontery.

"Yes, the devil usually takes the hindmost, so I've been told. Miss Larpent, anyway, is quite safe, for she will always be an easy first."

"There is such a thing as going too fast," commented Bunny.

"There is such a thing as getting away altogether," flung back Toby with spirit.

Bunny's eyes flashed into sudden, ominous flame. He could not have said why the contrast between the two girls, the one in her dainty summer attire and the other in her boyish riding-kit, had such an effect upon him, but for the moment it almost infuriated him.

Toby saw it, and her own eyes lit in response. She stood waiting for his rejoinder, the spirit of mischief incarnate, wary, alert, daring him.

But Bunny did not reply. He drew in a hard breath through teeth that gripped his lower lip and restrained himself. The next instant he had turned away.

"Oh, damn!" said Toby and swung upon her heel.

Saltash and the General walked beside her, rallying her. But Bunny and Sheila came behind in silence.

They found Maud awaiting them in the long, low room that overlooked her favourite view of the down. Saltash entered as one who had the right, and she greeted him with momentary surprise but evident pleasure.

"I couldn't spend twenty-four hours at Burchester without calling upon you," he said.

"You know you are always welcome," she answered.

They sat down by one of the wide French windows, and General Melrose began to occupy his hostess's attention. Sheila took a chair that Bunny pushed forward, and Saltash glanced round for Toby.

She was sitting on the end of a couch, playing with the silky ears of the old red setter. Her hat was flung down beside her, her pretty face downcast.

He crossed to her deliberately and bent also to fondle the dog.

She started slightly at his coming, and a faint flush rose in her cheeks, but she neither glanced at him nor spoke.

For the moment they were alone and unobserved by the laughing group at the window. Saltash bent suddenly lower. His quick whisper came down to her:

"Go and put on the most girlish thing you've got!"

She looked up at him then, her blue eyes seeking his. A rapid flash of understanding passed between them. Then without a word she rose.

When the tea was cold and forgotten, and Sheila was beginning to awake to the fact that it was growing late, there came a sudden, ringing laugh across the lawn, and Toby scampered into view with little Molly on her shoulder and Eileen running by her side.

She was dressed in white, and she looked no more than a child herself as she danced across the grass, executing a fairylike step as she came.

The tiny girl's tinkling laughter mingled with hers. Her little hands were fondly clasped about the girl's neck; she looked down into her face with babyish adoration, while Eileen, the elder child, gazed upward with a more serious devotion.

General Melrose interrupted his narrative to look at the advancing trio.

"By Jove, Mrs. Bolton, but that's a pretty sight!"

Sheila also ceased very suddenly to converse with Bunny, while Saltash made a scarcely perceptible movement as though he braced and restrained himself in the same instant.

"The prettiest picture I've seen for years!"

vowed the General. "How that little Larpent girl changes! She is like a piece of quicksilver. There's no getting hold of her. How old is she?"

"She is nearly twenty," said Bunny with the swiftness of ownership.

"Nearly twenty! You don't say so! She might be fourteen at the present moment. Look at that! Look at it!"

For Toby was suddenly whizzing like a butterfly across the lawn in a giddy flight that seemed scarcely to touch the ground, the little girl still upon her shoulder, the elder child standing apart and clapping her hands in delighted admiration.

"Yes, she is rather like fourteen," Maud said with her tender smile. "Ah, look! She is going to jump the sundial!"

Sheila turned to her.

"Surely you are nervous! If she fell, the little one might be terribly hurt."

"She won't fall," Maud said with confidence.

And even as she spoke, Toby leapt the sundial, leaving the ground as a bird leaves it, without effort or any sort of strain, and alighting again as a bird alights from a curving flight, with absolute freedom and a natural adroitness of movement indescribably pleasant to watch.

"A very pretty circus trick!" declared the General, and even Bunny's clouded brow cleared a little, though he said nothing.

"A circus trick, indeed!" said Sheila, as if speaking to herself. "How on earth did she do it?"

"She is like a boy in many ways," said Maud.

Sheila looked at her.

"Yes. She is just like a boy, or at least . . ."

Her look went further, reached Saltash, who

lounged on Maud's other side, and fell abruptly away.

As Toby came up with the two children, all of them flushed and laughing, Toby herself in her white frock looking like a child just out of school, she rose and turned to Bunny.

"We ought to go now," she said. "I am going to fetch the car round for Dad."

"I'll do it," he said.

But she went with him as he had known she would. They left the group at the window and moved away side by side in silence as they had walked that afternoon.

Saltash stood up and addressed Maud.

"I'm going too. Bunny is dining with me to-night. I suppose you won't come?"

She gave him her hand, smiling.

"I can't, thank you. Ask me another day! You and Bunny will really get on much better without me."

"Impossible!" he declared gallantly, but he did not press her.

He turned to the General and took his leave.

Toby and the two children walked the length of the terrace with him, all chattering at once. She seemed to be in a daring, madcap mood, and Saltash laughed and jested with her as though she had been indeed the child she looked.

Only at parting, when she would have danced away, he suddenly stopped her with a word.

"Nonette!"

She stood still, as if at a word of command; there had been something of compulsion in his tone.

He did not look at her, and the smile he

wore was wholly alien to the words he spoke.

"Be careful how you go! And don't see Bunny again till I have seen him!"

A hard breath went through Toby. She stood like a statue, the two children clasping her hands. Her blue eyes gazed at him with a wide questioning. Her face was white.

"Why? Why?" she whispered at length.

His look flashed before her vision like the grim play of a sword.

"That girl remembers you. She will give you away. She's probably at it now. I'll see him, tell him the truth if necessary. Anyhow—leave him to me!"

"Tell him . . . the truth?"

The words came from her like a cry. There was sudden terror in her eyes.

He made a swift gesture of dismissal.

"Go, child! Go! Whatever I do will make it all right for you. I'm standing by. Don't be afraid! Just . . . go!"

It was a definite command. She turned to obey, the little girls still clinging to her. The next moment she was running lightly back with them, and Saltash turned in the opposite direction and passed out of sight round the corner of the house on his way to the stable-yard.

Chapter
Nine

Saltash's spurs rang upon the white stones, and Sheila Melrose, standing beside her father's car in the shadow of some buildings, turned sharply and saw him.

Her face was pale; it had a strained expression. But it changed at sight of him. She regarded him with that look of frozen scorn which once she had flung him when they had met in the garish crowd at Valrosa.

Bunny was stooping over the car, but he became aware of Saltash almost in the same moment and stood up straight to face him.

Sheila was pale, but he was perfectly white, and there were heavy drops of perspiration on his forehead. He looked full at Saltash with eyes of blazing accusation.

Saltash's face never changed as he came up to the car.

"Car all right?" he asked smoothly. "Can I lend a hand? The General is beginning to move."

Sheila turned without a word and got into the car.

Bunny neither moved nor spoke. He stood like a man paralysed. It was Saltash who, with that royal air of amusing himself, stooped to the handle and started the engine.

The girl at the wheel did not even thank him. She looked beyond. Only as he stood aside and the car slid forward, she turned stiffly to Bunny.

"Good-bye!" she said.

He made a jerky movement. Their eyes met for a single second.

"You will write?" he said.

His throat was working spasmodically, the words seemed to come with gigantic effort. She bent her head in answer and passed between them through the white gate into the drive that led round to the house.

Saltash turned with a lightning movement to Bunny.

"Walk back with me and we can talk!"

Bunny drew sharply back. The movement was one of instinctive recoil. But still no words came. He stood staring at Saltash, and he was trembling from head to foot.

"Don't be an ass now!" Saltash said, and his voice was oddly gentle, even compassionate. "You've stumbled on a mare's nest. It's all right. I can explain."

But Bunny would not believe what Saltash told him about Toby and felt he was hiding something about her past.

He was shocked by what Sheila Melrose had told him, and he would not believe that Saltash had treated Toby as a boy. He felt there was more to it and that was why he was so anxious for him to marry her.

"I am going to her," he said, "to ask her for the whole truth—about her past."

"Is any woman capable of telling the truth to that extent?" questioned Saltash.

"I shall know if she doesn't," said Bunny doggedly.

"And will that help? Isn't it possible, sometimes, to try to know too much? There is such a thing as looking too closely, *mon ami*. And then we pay the price."

"Do you imagine I could ever be satisfied not knowing?" said Bunny.

Saltash shrugged his shoulders.

"I merely suggested that you are going the wrong way to satisfy yourself. But that is your affair, not mine. The gods have sent you a gift, and because you don't know what it is made of, you are going to pull it to pieces to find out.

"And presently you will fling it away because you cannot fit it together again. You don't realize, you never will realize, that the best things in life are the things we never see and only dimly understand."

"Do you mean to tell me," Bunny said, speaking slowly, "that you have never even tried to know where she came from—what she is?"

Saltash made a quick gesture as of remonstrance.

"*Mon ami,* the last I have always known. The first I have never needed to know."

"Then," Bunny spoke with difficulty, but his look never wavered, "tell me, as before God, tell me what you believe her to be!"

"What I know her to be," corrected Saltash, "I will tell you—certainly. She is a child who has looked into hell, but she is still . . . a child."

"What do you mean?" questioned Bunny.

Saltash's eyes suddenly flashed a direct challenge into his own.

"I mean that the flame has scorched her, but it has never actually touched her."

"You know that?" Bunny's voice was hoarse. There was torture in his eyes. "Man, for God's sake, the truth!"

"It is the truth," Saltash said.

"How do you know it? You've no proof. How can you be sure?"

He could not keep the anguish out of his voice. The words fell harsh and strained.

"How do I know it?" Saltash echoed the words sharply. "What proof? Bunny, you fool, do you know so little of the world, of women, as that? What proof do you need? Just look into her eyes!"

A queer note of passion sounded in his own voice as it told Bunny very clearly that he was grappling with the naked truth at last. It arrested him in a moment. He suddenly found that he could get no further. There was no need.

They parted almost without words a few minutes later. There was no more to be said.

*   *   *

After Saltash had dined that evening he went to his music-room. He passed through into the long, dim room beyond with its single red lamp burning at the far end.

He prepared to pass on to the door that led

out upon the gallery and so to the grand staircase. But before he had gone half-a-dozen paces he stopped.

It was no sound that arrested him, no visible circumstance of any sort. Yet, as if at a word of command, he halted.

His quick look swept around the room like the gleam of a rapier, and suddenly he swung upon his heel, facing that still, red light.

Seconds passed before he moved again. Then swiftly and silently he walked up the room. Close to the lamp was a deep settee on which the spots of a leopard-skin showed in weird relief.

At one end of the settee, against the leopard-skin, something gold was shining. Saltash's look was fixed upon it as he drew near.

He reached the settee, treading noiselessly. He stood beside it, looking down. And over his dark face with its weary lines and cynical mouth, its melancholy and its bitterness, there came a light such as neither man nor woman had ever seen upon it before.

For there before him, curled up like a tired puppy, her tumbled, golden hair lying in ringlets over the leopard-skin, was Toby, asleep in the dim, red lamplight.

For minutes he stood and gazed upon her before she awoke. For minutes that strange glory came and went over his watching face. He did not stir, did not seem even to breathe.

But the fact of his presence must have pierced her consciousness at last, for in the end, quite quietly, supremely naturally, the blue eyes opened and fixed upon him.

"Hullo!" said Toby sleepily. "Time to get up?"

And then, in a moment, she had sprung upright on the couch, swift dismay on her face.

"I . . . I thought we were on the yacht! I . . . I . . . I never meant to go to sleep here! I came to speak to you, Sir. I wanted to see you."

He put a restraining hand upon her thin young shoulder, and his touch vibrated as with some unknown force controlled.

"All right, Nonette!" he said, and his voice had the same quality; it was reassuring but oddly unsteady. "Sorry I kept you waiting."

She looked at him. Her face was quivering.

"I've had . . . a hell of a time. Been here hours . . . thought you'd never come."

He bent, put his hand under her elbow and helped her to her feet. She came up from the couch with a spring and stood before him, half daring and half shy.

"Are you . . . angry with me for coming?" she asked him quiveringly. "I . . . had to come."

He looked down into her eyes.

"*Bien, petite!* Then you need a friend."

Her answering look was piteous.

"I need . . . you."

One of the old gay smiles flashed across his face. He seemed to challenge her to lightness. The grimness went out of his eyes like a shadow.

"And so you have come, *ma mignonette,* at the dead of night . . . at the risk of your reputation —and mine . . ."

Toby made an excruciating grimace and broke impulsively in upon him.

"It wasn't the dead of night when I started. I have been waiting hours . . . hours. But it doesn't matter . . . it doesn't matter. I've found you . . . at last. And you can't send me away now ... like you did before ... because ... because ... well, I've no one to go to. You might have done it if you'd come down earlier. But you can't do it ... now."

Her voice thrilled on a high note of triumph.

"You've got to keep me ... now. I've come ... to stay."

"What?" said Saltash.

He bent towards her, looking closely into her face. "Got to keep you, have I? What's that mean? Has Bunny been a brute to you?"

"Bunny! I didn't wait to see him!"

"What?" Saltash said again.

She reached up a quick, nervous hand and laid it against his breast. Her eyes, wide and steadfast, never flinched from his.

"I've come ... to stay," she repeated.

And then, after a moment:

"It's all right. I left a note behind for Bunny. I told him ... I wasn't going back."

He caught her hand tightly into his. His hold was drawing her and she yielded herself to it still with that quivering laughter that was somehow more eloquent than words, more piteous than tears.

Saltash spoke below his breath.

"What am I going to do with you?"

Her arms reached up to him suddenly. Perhaps it was that for which she had waited.

"You're going ... to keep me ... this time," she told him tremulously. "Oh, why did you ever send me away ... when I belonged to you ... and to no one else? You meant to give me my chance?

What chance have I of anything but hell and damnation away from you? No, listen! Let me speak! Hear me first!"

She uttered the words with passionate insistence.

"I'm not asking anything of you ... only to be with you. I'll be to you whatever you choose me to be ... always ... always. I will be your valet, your slave, your ... plaything. I will be ... the dust under your feet. But I must be with you. You understand me. No one else does. No one else ever can."

"Are you sure you understand yourself?" Saltash said.

His arms closed about her. He was holding her in a vital clasp. But his restless look did not dwell upon her. It seemed rather to be seeking something beyond.

Toby's hands met and gripped each other behind his neck. She clung to him with an almost frenzied closeness.

"You can't send me away!" she told him brokenly. "If you do, I shall die. And I'm asking such a little, such a very little."

"You don't know what you're asking, child," he said, and though he held her fast-pressed to him his voice had the sombre ring of a man who battles with misgiving. "You never have known. That's the hell of it."

"I do know!" she flung back almost fiercely. "I know ... all I need to know ... of most things."

His look came swiftly to her. He made a sudden gesture of capitulation, and the strain went out of his look. His arms tightened like springs about her. He spoke lightly, jestingly.

"*Bien*! Shall I tell you what you shall be to me, *mignonne*?" he said and smiled down at her with his royal air of confidence.

She trembled a little and was silent, realizing that he had suddenly leapt to a decision, fearing desperately what that decision might be.

His old baffling mask of banter had wholly replaced the sombreness, but she was aware of a force behind it that gripped her irresistibly. She could not speak in answer.

"I will tell you," he said, and his dark face laughed into hers with a merriment half mischievous, half kindly. "I am treading the path of virtue, *mignonne,* and uncommon lonely I am finding it. You shall relieve the monotony. We will be virtuous together—for a while. You shall be ... my wife!"

He stooped with the words and before she knew it his lips were on her own. But his kiss, though tender, was as baffling as his smile. It was not the kiss of the lover.

She gasped and shrank away.

"Your ... wife! You ... you ... you are joking! How could I ... I ... be your wife?"

"You and none other!" he declared gaily. "Egad, it's the very thing for us! Why did I never think of it before? I will order the state-coach at once. We will go to town, elope, and be married before the world begins to buzz.

"What are you frightened at, sweetheart? Why this alarm? Wouldn't you rather be my wife than ... the dust beneath my feet?"

"I ... I don't know," faltered Toby and hid her face from the dancing raillery in his eyes.

His hold was close and sheltering, but he laughed at her without mercy.

"Does the prospect make you giddy? You will soon get over that. You will take the world by storm, *mignonne*. You will be the talk of the town."

"Oh, no!" breathed Toby. "No, I couldn't!"

"What?" he jested. "You are going to refuse my suit?"

She turned and clung to him with a passionate, even fierce intensity, but she did not lift her face again to his. Her voice came muffled against his breast.

"I could never refuse you . . . anything."

"Eh, bien! Then all is well!" he declared. "My bride will hold her own wherever she goes, save with her husband. And to him she will yield her wifely submission at all times. Do you know what they will say, all of them, when they hear that Charles Rex is married at last?"

"What?" whispered Toby apprehensively.

He bent his head, still laughing.

"Shall I tell you? Can't you guess?"

"No. Tell me!" she said.

He touched the soft ringlets of her hair with his lips.

"They will say, 'God help his wife!' *mignonne.* And I, I shall answer 'Amen.' "

She lifted her face suddenly and defiantly, her eyes afire.

"Do you know what I shall say if they do?"

"What?" said Saltash, his own eyes gleaming oddly.

"I shall tell them," said Toby tensely, "to . . . to . . . to go to blazes!"

He grimaced his appreciation.

"Then they will begin to pity the husband, *chérie*."

She held up her lips to him childishly, lovingly.

"I will be good. I will be good. I will never say such things again."

He kissed the trembling lips again, lightly, caressingly.

"Oh, don't be too good! I couldn't live up to it. You shall say what you like—do what you like. And you shall be my Queen!"

She caught back another sob. Her clinging arms tightened.

"And you will be . . . what you have always been . . . my King . . . my King . . . my King!"

In the silence that followed the passionate words, Charles Rex very gently loosened the clinging arms and set her free.

* * *

"I never thought it would be like this," Toby exclaimed.

She spoke aloud though she was alone. She stood at an immense window on the first floor of a busy Paris hotel and stared down into the teeming courtyard below.

At the opening of a door in the room behind her, she turned very swiftly, and in a moment her face was alight with ardent welcome.

"Ah! Here you are!" she said.

He came forward in his quick, springy fashion, his eyes laughing their gay greeting into hers. He took the hands she held out to him and, bending lightly, kissed them.

"Have you been bored? *Mais non!* I have not been so long gone. Why are you not still resting, *chérie,* as I told you?"

"I am . . . quite rested, *Monseigneur.* And the tiredness . . . quite gone. And now you are going to take me to see the sights of Paris?"

"Those of them you don't know?" suggested Saltash.

She nodded.

"I don't know very many. I never went very far. I was afraid."

He twisted his hand through her arm, and his fingers closed upon her wrist.

"You are not afraid with me?"

"Never, *Monseigneur.*"

"Why do you call me that?" said Saltash.

She coloured at the abrupt question.

"It suits you."

He made his monkeyish grimace and suddenly dropped his eyes to the blue-veined wrist in his grasp.

"Are you happy, *mignonne?*" he asked her, still obviously in a jesting mood.

Toby's eyes dropped also. She mutely nodded.

"The truth, Nonette?" His look flashed over her, his tone was imperious.

She nodded again.

"I always tell you . . . the truth."

He began to laugh.

"*Mais vraiment!* I had not thought that likely. Then you do not want to leave me yet?"

"Leave you!" Her eyes came up to his in wide amazement. "I!"

"We have been married three days," he reminded her with comically working brows. "And have I not already begun to leave you, to neglect you?"

"I . . . I . . . I never expected . . . anything else," stammered Toby, suddenly averting her face.

He patted her cheek with careless kindliness.

"How wise of you, my dear! How wise! Then you are not yet sufficiently *ennuyée* to desire to leave me?"

"Why . . . why do you ask?" questioned Toby.

There was a species of malicious humour about him that made her uneasy. Saltash in a mischievous mood was not always easy to restrain. He did not immediately reply to her question, and she turned with a hint of panic and tightly clasped his arm.

"It is . . . you who are . . . *ennuyé!*" she said with piteous eyes upraised.

He flicked her cheek with his thumb, his odd eyes gleaming.

"Not so, *miladi* Saltash! For me the game is but just begun. But should you desire to leave me, the opportunity is yours. A knight has arrived to the rescue, a very puissant knight!"

"A knight!" gasped Toby, trembling. "Ah! Tell me what you mean?"

His look was openly mocking.

"A knight in gaiters!" he told her lightly. "A knight who bears or should bear a horsewhip in place of a sword—that is, if I know him aright!"

"Jake!" she gasped incredulously.

He laughed afresh.

"Even so! Jake! Most worthy and most obtrusive! What shall we do with him, lady mine? Slay him—or give him a feed and send him home?"

She stared at him, aghast.

"You . . . you . . . you are joking!" she stammered.

"I always joke when I am most serious," Saltash assured her.

"Oh, don't!" She clung closer to his arm. "What shall we do? He . . . he can't do anything, can he? We . . . we . . . we really are married, aren't we?"

Saltash's most appalling grimace fled like a hunted goblin across his face.

"Married? Heavens, child! What more do you want? Haven't you seen it, actually seen it, in our great London daily? And can a London daily lie? You may have dreamed the wedding, but that paragraph, that paragraph, it takes a genius of the first literary degree to dream a paragraph, though it may only need quite an ordinary fool to write it!"

"Don't let him take me away!" she besought him shakily. "You . . . you . . . you've promised to keep me . . . now."

"But of course I'm keeping you." Saltash laughed. "It's what I did it for. It's the very essence of the game. Cheer up, Nonette! I'm not parting with any of my goods, worldly or otherwise, this journey."

"You are sure?" whispered Toby. "Sure?"

"Sure of what?" He bent swiftly and, for a second, only a second, his lips touched her hair.

"Sure you . . . don't . . . want to?" came in a gasp from Toby as she burrowed a little deeper.

"Oh, that!" Saltash stood up again and his face was sardonic, for the moment almost grim.

"Yes, quite sure of that, my dear. Moreover, it will amuse me to meet the virtuous Jake on his own ground for once. A new sensation, Nonette!

"Will you help me to face him? Or do you prefer the more early-Victorian *rôle* of the lady who retires till the combat is over and then emerges to reward the winner?"

She lifted her head at that and uttered a scoffing little laugh, withdrawing herself abruptly from his support. Her pointed chin went up with a hint of defiance. All signs of agitation were gone.

"I'll stay and help you," she said.

He made her an elaborate bow.

"Then we will ring up the curtain. I congratulate you, Madam, upon your spirit."

*   *   *

When finally Jake left after satisfying himself Toby was happy, Saltash told her he had something for her.

"What is it?" Toby asked.

Her bright eyes questioned him. She looked more than ever like an eager boy. He pulled a leather case out of his pocket and held it out to her.

"Oh, what is it?" she said and coloured more deeply. "You haven't . . . haven't . . . been buying me things!"

"Open it!" said Saltash with regal peremptoriness.

But still she hesitated till he suddenly laid his hands on hers and compelled her. She saw a single string of pearls on a bed of blue velvet. Her eyes came up to his in quick distress.

"Oh, I ought not to take them!" she said.

"And why not?" said Saltash.

She bit her lip, almost as if she would burst into tears.

"Monseigneur . . ."

"Call me Charles!" he commanded.

His hands still held hers. She dropped her eyes to them and suddenly, very suddenly, she bent her head and kissed them.

He started slightly and in a moment he set her free, leaving the case in her hold.

"Eh, bien! That is understood. You like my pearls, *chérie?"*

"I love . . . anything . . . that comes from you," she replied softly. "But these . . . but . . . these . . . I ought not to take these."

"But why not?" he questioned. "May I not make you a present? Are you not my wife?"

"Yes." More faintly came Toby's answer. "But . . . but . . . but a wife is different. A wife . . . does not need . . . presents."

"Mais vraiment!" protested Saltash. "So a wife is different. How different, *mignonne?"*

He tried to look into the downcast eyes, but she would not raise them. She was trembling a little.

"Such things as these," she said under her breath, "are what a man would give to . . . to . . . to the woman he loves."

"And so you think they are unsuitable for my wife?" questioned Saltash with a whimsical look on his dark face.

She did not answer him, only mutely held out the case, still without looking at him.

He stood for a second or two, watching her, an odd flame coming and going in his eyes; then abruptly he moved, picked up the pearls from their case, straightened them dexterously, and clasped them about her neck.

She lifted her face then, quivering and irresolute, to his.

"And I can give you . . . nothing!"

He took her lightly by the shoulders, as one who caresses a child.

"*Ma chérie,* you have given me already much more than you realize. But we will not go into that now. We will go to the shops. Afterwards, we will go out to Fontainebleau and picnic in the forest. You will like that?"

"Oh, so much!" she said with enthusiasm.

Yet there was a puzzled look of pain in her eyes as she turned away, and though she wore his pearls she made no further reference to them.

*   *   *

It was dark when they returned to the hotel, but Paris shone with a million lights. The hotel itself had a festive air. There were flowers in all directions, and a red carpet had been laid upon the steps.

"Rozelle Daubeni is expected," said Saltash.

"Who?" Toby stopped short in the act of descending.

Her face shone white in the glare. A moment before she had been lauging, but the laugh went into her question with a little choked sound.

"Who did you say?" she questioned more coherently.

"*Mademoiselle* Daubeni—the idol of Paris. Never heard of her?" Saltash handed her lightly down. "She is coming to dance in the great *salon* tonight. You shall see her. She is a thing to re-member."

Toby gave a quick shiver.

"Yes, I have heard of her too much . . . too much! I don't want to see her. Shall we dine up-stairs?"

"Oh, I think not," said Saltash with decision. "You are too retiring, *ma chère*. It doesn't become a lady of your position."

He followed her towards the lift. The vesti-bule was full of people, laughing and talking, awaiting the coming of the favourite.

But as the girl in her blue cloak went through, a sudden hush fell. Women lifted glasses to look at her and men turned to watch.

Saltash sauntered behind her in his regal way, looking neither to right nor left, yet fully aware of all he passed. No one accosted him.

There were times when even those who knew him well would have hesitated to do so. He could surround himself with an atmosphere so suavely impersonal as to be quite impenetrable to all.

It surrounded him now. He walked like a king through a crowd of courtiers, and the buzz of talk did not spring up again till he was out of sight.

"So you do not want to see *la première dan-seuse du siècle!*" he commented as he entered the sitting-room of their suite behind Toby.

She turned, blue eyes wide with protest in her white face.

"Do you wish me to see her, My Lord? That . . . woman!"

He frowned upon her suddenly.

"Call me Charles! Do you hear? We will play this game according to rule—or not at all."

"You are angry," Toby said and turned still whiter.

He came to her, thrust a quick arm about her.

"I am not angry, *mignonne*, at least not with you. But you must take your proper place. I can't keep you in hiding here. Those gaping fools downstairs, they have got to understand. You are not my latest whim, but a permanent institution. You are . . . my wife."

She shivered in his hold, but she clung to him.

"I don't feel like a permanent institution," she told him rather piteously. "And when you are angry . . ."

"I am not angry," said Saltash and tweaked her ear as though she had been a boy. "But whether you feel like it or not, you are my wife, and you have got to play the part. *C'est entendu, n'est-ce pas?*"

"Whatever you wish," said Toby faintly.

He set her free.

"You must look your best tonight. Wear blue! It is your colour. I shall present Spentoli to you. And tomorrow he will want to paint you."

Toby stiffened.

"That . . . *canaille!*"

He looked at her in surprise.

"What is the matter with you tonight, Nonette? You are hating all the world."

Her blue eyes blazed.

"I don't want to meet Spentoli. He has an evil eye. You . . . you . . . I look to you to . . . to . . . to protect me."

"My good child!" Saltash exclaimed.

He turned aside to light a cigarette and there

was a pause. But Toby still stood rigid, as it were on guard. He spoke again after a moment, and his voice was kind though it had a certain dominant quality also.

"Nonette, you need not be afraid when you are with me. I shall protect you. Now go and dress! When you are ready, come to me for inspection! And remember! You are to look your best tonight."

He turned with the last words and looked at her. His brows went up as he realized her attitude, the tense resistance of the slight figure withstanding him.

But it was only for a moment or two that the girl maintained her stand. Seeing the look that leapt into his eyes her own were swiftly lowered. She drew back from him.

"I will do ... whatever you wish," she said again nervously. "You know that."

"Yes, I know that," said Saltash with his quick grimace. "You have my sympathy, Nonette. Now go, *ma chère,* go!"

She went from his presence like a small, hunted animal.

Saltash shrugged his shoulders and sauntered down again to the vestibule. The crowd had grown. They were watching the great entrance-door expectantly for the coming of the celebrated dancer. Saltash called for a drink and mingled with the throng.

The Italian, Spentoli, came up presently and joined him.

"I am hoping that you will presently give me the great honour of presenting me to your bride."

Saltash looked at him.

"My wife is young and shy," he said after a moment. "I will present you, some day, Spentoli, but it may not be yet."

"I did not think you would marry one so young." Spentoli smiled. "She has the athletic look of a boy. She reminds me . . ."

"Of a picture called 'The Victim' by one . . . Spentoli!" Saltash's voice was suave. "A cruel picture, *mon ami,* but of an amazing merit. I have seen the likeness also. Where did you get it?"

The Italian was still smiling, but his eyes were wary.

"From a little circus-rider in California—a child, an imp of a child, astonishingly clever, a wisp of inspiration. Yes, a girl of course, but she had all the lines of a boy, the perfect limbs of an athlete.

"I took her from her circus. I should have paid her well had she remained with me. But before the picture was finished she was tired. She was a little serpent, wily and wicked.

"One day we had a small discussion in my studio, oh, quite a small discussion. And she stuck her poison-fang into me—and fled."

Spentoli's teeth gleamed through his black moustache.

"I do not like these serpent-women. When I meet her again, it will be my turn to strike."

"Our turn so seldom comes," said Saltash lazily, his eyes wandering to the door. "*Mademoiselle* Rozelle, for instance, would hold her own against any of us."

"Ah! Rozelle!" Spentoli's face changed magically. "But she is beautiful and without venom, a rose without a thorn!"

There came the sound of a laugh, a clear, ringing laugh, childishly, irresistibly gay, and a figure in blue came in through the marble pillars.

As a queen they had prepared for her, and as a queen she entered, a being so exquisite, so goddess-like, that every breath was drawn in wonder.

She looked around her with eyes that shone like sapphires. Her red lips were parted. She had the expectant look of girlhood, yet her beauty had a quality unknown to youth. And it was to that quality, almost unknown to himself, that Saltash did homage as he rose.

Her look flashed across to him, comprehended his action, and laughed open triumph. Then with a suddenness almost too swift to follow, she turned to a man who had entered behind her and softly spoke.

Saltash's eyes went to the man, and he drew a low whistle between his teeth. It was well known that Rozelle Daubeni never travelled without an escort; but this man—this man!

He was tall and broad and he carried himself with a supreme contempt for his fellow-men. He did not look at Saltash, did not apparently even see the hushed crowd that hung upon every movement of that wonderful woman-creature who took the world by storm wherever she went.

He was superbly indifferent to his surroundings, gazing straight before him with the eyes of a Viking who searches the far horizon. He walked with the free swing of a pirate. And as the woman turned her dazzling face towards him, it was plain to all that she saw none but him in that vast and crowded place.

He was by her side as they moved forward,

and they saw her lightly touch his arm with an intimate gesture, as though they were alone. Then the whole throng broke into acclamations and the spell was broken.

She saw them all again and laughed her gracious thanks. The great hall rang with their greeting as she passed through, but no one sought to detain her and she did not pause.

Later she would give them all they desired, but her moment had not arrived. So she went on to the great curving staircase, side by side with her fair-bearded Viking, still laughing like a happy child who looks for the morrow.

As she rounded the curve of the stair she snatched a red rose from her breast and threw it down to her worshippers below.

It was aimed at Saltash, but it fell before Spentoli, and he caught and held it with wild adoration leaping in his eyes. As he pressed it to his lips he was sobbing.

"Mon ami," said Saltash's voice behind him, maliciously humorous, "you have stolen my property. But since I have no use for it, you may keep it."

Spentoli looked at him with burning eyes.

"Ah! You may laugh!" he said in a fierce undertone. "You are without a soul."

"Isn't it better to laugh?" queried Saltash. "Did you expect a blow in the face?"

Spentoli glared for a moment and recovered himself.

"Do you know what they are saying of her? They say that she is dying. But it is not true—not true! Such beauty as that, such loveliness, could never die!"

The cynical lines in Saltash's face deepened very perceptibly. He shrugged his shoulders and said nothing.

"Who is the man with her?" demanded Spentoli. "I have never seen him before, the man with the face of a Dane. Do you know him?"

"Yes, I know him," said Saltash.

"Then who is he? Some new lover?"

There was suppressed eagerness in the question. Spentoli's eyes were smouldering again.

Saltash was looking supremely ironical.

"Perhaps new. More likely very old. His name is Larpent, and he is the captain of my yacht."

Chapter
Ten

"We will watch from the gallery," Saltash said.

Toby looked up at him with quick gratitude. "There won't be so many people there."

He frowned at her, but his look was quizzical.

"But everyone will know that Lady Saltash is present, with her husband."

She slipped a persuasive hand on to his arm.

"King Charles, let us leave Paris!"

"Bored?" said Saltash.

Her face was slightly drawn. "No . . . no! Only . . ." She paused, then suddenly flashed him her swift smile. "Let it be as you wish!"

He flicked her cheek in his careless, caressing way.

"Shall I tell you something, *mignonne*? We are going—very soon."

Her eyes shone, more blue than the frock she wore. She stooped impulsively and touched his hand with her lips then, as though she feared to anger him, drew quickly away.

"Shall we go on the yacht?" she asked, eagerness half suppressed in her voice.

"Yes," said Saltash, and he spoke with finality, even with a certain grimness.

Toby's face lighted up for a second and then clouded again. She glanced at him doubtfully.

"If Paris amuses you . . ." she ventured.

"Paris does not amuse me," said Saltash emphatically. "Have a cigarette, *ma chère*, while I go and dress!"

When they went down to the great *salle à manger* a little later, her face was flushed and her smile ready, though she glanced about her in a shy, half-furtive fashion as they entered.

They found a secluded table reserved for them in a corner, and her eyes expressed relief. She shrank into it as if she would make herself as small as possible.

Again no one accosted them, though a good many looked in their direction. Saltash was far too well known a figure to pass unnoticed in any fashionable crowd.

But the general attention did not centre upon them. That was absorbed by a far greater attraction that night.

She sat at the end of the room like a queen holding her court, and beside her sat the Viking, stern-faced and remote of mien, as supremely isolated as though he sat with her on a desert island.

He spoke but seldom, and then to her exclusively. But when he spoke she turned to him the radiant face of the woman who holds within her grasp her heart's desire.

After dinner Saltash and Toby passed out

through the throng of diners almost unobserved, but in the corridor Spentoli leaned against a pillar smoking a long, black cigar.

He made no movement to intercept them, but his eyes with their restless fire dwelt upon the girl in a fashion that drew her own irresistibly. She saw him and slightly paused.

It was the pause of the hunted animal that sees its retreat cut off, but in an instant Saltash's voice, very cool, arrogantly self-assured, checked the impulse to panic.

"Straight on to the lift, *ma chère*! See! It is there in front of you. There will be no one in the gallery. Go straight on!"

She obeyed him instinctively as her habit was, but in the lift she trembled so much that he made her sit down. He stood beside her in silence, but once lightly his hand touched her cheek.

She moved then swiftly, convulsively, and caught it in both her own. But the next moment he had gently drawn it free.

The gallery that ran round three sides of the great *salon* was deserted. There was only one point at the far end where a view of the stage that had been erected for the dancer could be obtained. Towards this Saltash turned.

"We shall see her from here," he said.

The place was but dimly illuminated by the flare of the many lights below, two great crystal candelabra that hung at each end being left unlighted. Under one of these was a settee which Saltash drew forward to the balcony.

Very soon the *salon* was full of people and the lights were lowered there, while on the stage

only a single shaft of blinding violet light re-
mained, shooting downwards from the centre.
Toby's eyes became fixed upon that shaft of light.
She seemed to have forgotten to breathe.

The band had ceased to play. There fell a
potent silence. The multitude below sat motionless,
as if beneath a spell. And then she came.

No one saw her coming. She arrived quite
suddenly as though she had slid down that shaft
of light. And she was there before them dancing,
dancing like a winged thing in the violet radiance.

Not a sound broke the stillness save a single,
wandering thread of melody that might have come
from the throat of a bird, soft, fitful, but half awake
in the dawning.

Up in the gallery Toby drew a deep breath, as
of one coming out of a trance, and turned towards
the man beside her. The light had been turned on
in the *salon* below, and it struck upwards on her
face, showing it white and weary.

"So she has found another victim!" she said.

"It seems so," said Saltash.

She looked at him in the dimness.

"Did you know that . . . that Captain Larpent
was with her?"

"No," said Saltash.

He leaned forward abruptly, meeting her look
with a sudden challenge.

"Did you?"

She drew back sharply.

"Of course not! Of course not! What . . . what
should I know about her?"

He leaned back again without comment and
lighted another cigarette.

At the end of several seconds of silence

Toby spoke again, her locked fingers pulling against each other nervously.

"I wonder . . . do you mind . . . if I go soon? I . . . I am rather tired."

The lights went out as she spoke and Saltash's face became invisible. He spoke quite kindly, but with decision, out of the darkness.

"After this dance, *ma chère*—if you desire it."

The music began, weird and mournful, and a murmur went round among the eager watchers. It was her most famous dance, the Dance of Death, the most gruesome spectacle, so it was said, that any dancer had ever conceived.

She came on to the stage like the flash of an arrow, dressed in black that glittered and scintillated with every amazing movement. And then it began, the most wonderful dance of hers that all the world was mad to see.

Those who saw that dance of Rozelle Daubeni never forgot it, and there was hardly a woman in the audience who was not destinted to shudder whenever the memory of it arose.

It was arresting, revolting, terrible, yet compelling. A good many began to sob with the sheer nervous horror of it, yearning for the end upon which they were forced to look, though with a dread that made the blood run cold.

But the end was such as no one in that assembly looked for, just as the awful ecstasy of the dance was at its height; just as she lifted her face in the last anguish of supplication, yielding the last hope, sinking in nerveless surrender before the implacable destroyer, there came a sudden flare of light in the *salon*.

And the great crystal candelabra that hung

over the end of the gallery where the man and the girl were seated watching became a dazzling sparkle of overwhelming light.

Everyone turned towards it instinctively, and Toby, hardly knowing what she did, but with the instinct to escape strong upon her, leapt to her feet.

In that moment, as she stood in the full light, the dancer's eyes also shot upwards and saw the slim young figure. It was only for a moment, but instantly a wild cry rang through the great *salon,* a cry of agony so piercing that women shrieked and trembled, hiding their faces from they knew not what.

In the flash of a second the light was gone, the gallery again in darkness. But on the stage a woman's voice cried thrice:

"Toinette! Toinette! Toinette!" in the anguished accents of a mother who cries for her dead child, and then fell into a tragic silence more poignant than any sound, a silence that was as the silence of Death.

And in that silence a man's figure, moving with the free, athletic swing of a sailor, crossed the stage to where the dancer lay huddled in the dimness like a broken thing, lifted her and bore her away.

*   *   *

Very late that night, when all the crowds who had assembled to watch Rozelle Daubeni had dispersed with awe-struck whisperings, two men came down the great staircase into the empty vestibule and paused at the foot.

"You are leaving Paris again?" said Saltash.

The other nodded, his face perfectly emotionless, his eyes the eyes of the sailor who searches the far horizon.

"There is nothing to keep me here. I have always hated towns. I only came . . ."

He stopped, considered a moment, and said no more.

Saltash's eyes were upon him, alert, speculative, but wholly without malice.

"You came because you were sent for."

Larpent nodded twice thoughtfully, more as if in answer to some mental suggestion than as if the words had been actually uttered.

"There was only one reason on earth that would have brought me."

"Yes," said Saltash.

He dropped into a chair with the air of a man who has limitless leisure at his disposal, but his tone was casual. He did not ask for confidence.

Larpent stood, still gazing before him through the smoke with keen, unwavering eyes.

"Only one reason," he said again, and still he seemed to speak as one who communes with his inner soul. "She was dying, and she wanted me."

He paused a moment, and an odd tremor went through him.

"After twenty years," he said, as if in wonder at himself.

Saltash's look came swiftly upwards.

"I've heard that before. Those she caught she kept—always. No other woman was ever worth while after Rozelle."

Larpent's hands clenched instinctively, but he said nothing.

Saltash went on in the same casual tone.

"She never caught me, *mon ami*. I met her too late in life, when I was beginning to get fastidious. I appreciated her charm, but . . . it left me cold."

"You never saw her in her first youth," said Larpent, and into his fixed eyes there came a curious glow, the look of a man who sees a vision.

"What was she like then?" said Saltash.

"She was like a butterfly that plays among the flowers in the early morning. She had the look of a boy, the wide-open eyes, the fearless way, the freedom, the daring. Her innocence, her loveliness . . ."

Something rose unexpectedly in his throat. He stopped and swallowed hard.

"My God! How lovely she was, and I was . . . her husband."

"What?" said Saltash.

Larpent paced on with bent head.

"I was her husband. But I was at sea and she was on shore. And so I lost her."

"And yet you loved her?" Saltash said with a queer twist of the features that was not of mirth.

"I loved her, yes. If I hadn't loved her I would never have come to her when she called. That is love—the thing that doesn't die."

A sudden throb sounded in Larpent's voice. He paused for a moment in his walk, then paced on.

"You may laugh at it, call it what you will, but there is a power on the earth that is stronger than anything else, and when that power speaks we have got to obey. I didn't want to come. You think me a damn fool for coming, but I had to. That's all there is to it."

"I don't think you any sort of a fool," Saltash threw in briefly. "You did the only thing possible."

"Yes, the only thing. I came to her. If I hadn't come she'd have died—alone. But that alone wasn't why she sent for me; it was the primary reason, but not the only one. There was another."

Larpent ceased his pacing and deliberately faced the man who stood listening.

"You know what happened tonight. That child—the scaramouch you picked out of the gutter at Valrosa—Toby, do you realize—have you grasped—the meaning of that yet?"

Saltash flung up his head with an arrogant gesture.

"There is one thing about her you have not grasped. But go on! I may as well hear it."

"When I came to her yesterday she told me of a child that had been born to her, a child she had loved but had been unable to protect. It was a long story. Spentoli, the Italian artist, knows it from beginning to end. You know Spentoli?"

"I know him," said Saltash.

"Spentoli is a blackguard," Larpent said, "the sort that is born, not made afterwards. He has painted Rozelle over and over again. He may be a genius. He is certainly mad. He wanted the child for a model, and Rozelle could not prevent it. So she told me. I believe she was dependent upon him at the time.

"And so he had the child, but only for a time. The girl had a will of her own and broke away, joined a circus in California. He tracked her down, captured her again, tried to make a slave of her. But she was like a wild creature. She stabbed him one night and fled. That was Rozelle's trouble. She had never been able to hear of her again.

"She begged me to find and save her. I promised to do my best. But there was no need to search very far. Tonight Spentoli pulled the wires again. It was he who switched on that light. It was he who killed Rozelle.

"The girl in the gallery with you, Toby, was her daughter—and mine. You heard Rozelle cry out when she saw her. She never spoke again."

Larpent ceased to speak. He was no longer looking at Saltash. The far vision seemed to have caught his gaze again. He stared beyond.

But when Saltash told him Toby was now his wife he was delighted. Larpent's hand came out to him abruptly.

"It's the best thing you've ever done, My Lord," he said. "And you will never regret it."

"What makes you say that?" said Saltash curiously.

Their hands gripped and fell apart. Larpent answered him in the brief fashion of the man whose words are few:

"Mainly because you loved her enough to marry her when you could have had her without."

Saltash's laugh had the old derisive ring, but there was no corresponding gleam of mockery in his eyes as he turned carelessly aside.

"What is this thing called love?"

* * *

After Jake left Saltash he decided to visit some old friends in Paris.

Eventually he dined at a restaurant and then went to the station to catch the night train to Calais.

Walking solidly down the platform he found an empty carriage and threw his belongings on to a seat. He had some minutes to wait, and he lighted his pipe and began to pace the platform unencumbered.

He had strolled almost to the barrier and was in the act of turning back when something, some impulse for which he could never afterwards account, induced him to pause and take stock of the passengers passing through.

The train was almost due to start, and there was some slight confusion and a quickening of feet on the platform.

He realized that he ought to be going back to his own carriage, but something stayed him. He stood still, his keen eyes searching the hastening figures.

In a moment his attention was focussed upon a girl in a blue cloak who came towards him at a run, evidently intent upon catching the train.

She passed him swiftly without seeing him, almost brushed against him. And behind her came a dark man with black moustache and imperial, following her closely with an air of proprietorship.

Jake wheeled in his tracks, for a second amazed out of all composure. But an instant later he was in pursuit.

He had had but a fleeting glimpse of her face, and the blue cloak was quite unfamiliar to him; but there was no mistaking the boyish freedom of her gait, the athletic swing of her, as she turned and leapt into a compartment that her companion opened for her.

The black-browed Italian was in the act of following when Jake arrived. The realization of another hand upon the door was the first intimation that reached him of the Englishman's presence.

He turned and looked into a pair of red-brown eyes that regarded him with the utmost steadiness as a quiet voice made slightly drawling explanation.

"This lady is a friend of mine," said Jake Bolton. "I should like a word with her."

The Italian looked murderous for a moment, but he gave ground almost in spite of himself. Perhaps the calm insistence of the other man's bearing warned him at the outset of the futility of attempting any other course of action.

Jake was actually in the carriage before he could jerk out a word of protest.

"*Sapristi!* You go too far!" he blustered then.

But Jake was already confronting the girl, who had started up at his coming, and stood facing him white and shaken. He spoke, still quite quietly, even gently, but in the tone that no delinquent ever heard unmoved.

"Say," he said, "are you playing the game?"

She put up a hand to her throat. His sudden coming had unnerved her and she had no words. But her quivering face and tragic eyes were more than sufficient answer for Jake.

He had dealt with sudden emergencies before, and he treated this one with characteristic decision.

"You've no business here," he said, "and you know it. If you can't stick to the man you've married, come home with me to Maud!"

She made a sharp gesture towards him, as if on the verge of falling, and as sharply recovered herself.

"Oh, I wish . . . how I wish I could!"

Jake's hand, perfectly steady, full of sustaining strength, closed with authority upon her arm.

"That's settled then. Come now!"

But at this point the Italian burst furiously in upon them with a flood of unintelligible language that made all further speech impossible.

Jake glanced momentarily over his shoulder, as if disturbed by the buzzing of some insect, then with unruffled composure turned back to the girl.

His eyes looked straight into hers for perhaps ten seconds, then in the same purposeful fashion he set her free and deliberately turned upon the man who raged behind him.

As he did so there came a shouting and banging of doors along the platform, and the train began to move. Jake's massive shoulders braced themselves.

Without words he seized the raving Italian in a grip there was no resisting, swept him, as a sudden gale sweeps a leaf, across the compartment, sent him with a neat twist buzzing forth upon the platform, and very calmly shut the door and came back.

Then there came a wild shriek of laughter from Toby, and she doubled up in her corner with hysterical mirth, gasping and gasping for breath, till he sat squarely down beside her and pulled her into the circle of his arm.

"Easy, my girl! Easy!" he said. "We're not going to have an exhibition at this stage. You keep a stiff upper lip till you feel better!"

But the stiff upper lip was rather painfully lacking on that occasion. She very soon ceased to laugh, but for a long time thereafter she lay sobbing and shuddering like a little terrified animal against his breast, while the train rushed on through the night.

He was very gentle with her. Jake's stock of patience was practically limitless, and he and Toby had always had a certain comradeship between them, but finally she became quiet.

*　　*　　*

"It's been a funny game," said Saltash with a wry grimace. "We've both of us been so damned subtle that it seems to me we've ended up in much the same sort of hole that we started in."

"But you're not going to stay in it," said Maud.

He turned and looked down at her, one eyebrow cocked at a comic angle.

"*Ma belle reine,* if you can help us to climb out, you will earn my undying gratitude."

She met his look with her steadfast eyes.

"Charlie, do you know that night after night she cries as if her poor little heart were broken?"

"*Mais pourquoi?* I have not broken it. I have never even made love to her."

"Perhaps that is why. She is so young . . . so forlorn . . . and so miserable. Is it quite impossible for you to forgive her?"

"Forgive her!" said Saltash. "Does she want to be forgiven?"

"She is fretting herself ill over it," Maud replied. "I can't bear to see her. No, she has told me nothing except that she is waiting for you to throw her off, to divorce her. Charlie, you wouldn't do that even if you could!"

Saltash was silent, the scowl still upon his face.

She watched him with puzzled eyes, his face full of mocking humour.

"Now tell me!" she said. "How can I help you?"

He made a wide gesture.

"I leave that entirely to your discretion, Madam. As you may perceive, I have wholly ceased to attempt to help myself."

"You are not angry with her?" she hazarded.

"I am furious," said Charles Rex royally.

"You're not in earnest, and it wouldn't help you if you were. Besides, you couldn't be angry with the poor little thing. Charlie, you love her, don't you? You . . . you want her back."

"Do I want her back?" he said. "On my oath, it's hard to tell."

"Oh, surely!" Maud said.

She rose impulsively and stood beside him.

"Charlie, why do you wear a mask with me? Do you think I don't know that she is all the world to you?"

"There is no woman on this earth that I can't do without," he said. "I learnt that—when I lost you."

"Ah!" Maud's voice was very pitiful.

Her hand came to his.

"But this . . . this is different. Why should you do without her? You know she loves you?"

His fingers closed springlike about her own. A certain hardness was in his look.

"If she loves me, she can come back to me of her own accord."

"But if she is afraid?" Maud pleaded.

"She has no reason to be," he said. "I have claimed nothing from her. I have never spoken a harsh word to her. Why is she afraid?"

"Have you understood her?" Maud asked very gently.

He made an abrupt movement as though the question, notwithstanding the absolute kindness of its utterance, had somehow an edge for him.

He surprised her eventually by turning the talk to his new yacht, and very abruptly he announced his intention of going round the world in her.

"Not alone?" she said, and then would have checked the words lest they should seem to ask too much.

But he answered her without a pause.

"Yes, alone. And if I don't come back, Bunny can marry Toby and reign here in my stead. That is, if he isn't an infernal fool. If he is, then Toby can reign here alone, with you and Jake to take care of her."

"But, Charlie, why . . . why?"

The words leapt from Maud in spite of her.

"They've always cared for one another. Don't you know it? It's true she put me in a shrine and worshipped me for a time, but I couldn't live up to it. *Figurez-vous, ma chère!* Myself, a marble saint!"

"You never understood her," Maud said.

He shrugged his shoulders and went lightly on.

"Oh, she was ready enough to offer me human sacrifice, but that wasn't enough for me. Besides, I didn't want sacrifice. I have stood between her and the world. I have given her protection. But it was a free gift. I don't take anything in exchange for that."

An odd note sounded in his voice, as of some emotion suppressed. He leaned back against the window-frame, his hands behind his head.

"That wasn't what I married her for. I tried to prove that to her. I actually thought that I could win her trust like any ordinary man. I failed, of course—failed hideously.

"She never expected decent treatment from me. She never even began to trust me. I was far too heavily handicapped for that. And so as soon as the wind changed, the boat capsized."

"What made the wind change?" Maud asked gently.

He looked across at her, the baffling smile still in his eyes.

"The gods played a jest with us. It was only a small jest, but it turned the scale. She fled. That was how I came to realize I couldn't hold her. I had travelled too fast as usual, and she couldn't keep up.

"Well," he unlocked his hands and straightened himself, "it's up to Bunny now. I'll let her go to him."

"My dear!" Maud said.

He laughed at her with the old, half-caressing ridicule. "That shocks you? But why, if they love each other?"

Maud rose quickly. There was something in his attitude or expression that she could not bear.

"Oh, you are wrong! You are wrong! You have the power to make her love you. And you love her. Charlie, this thing has not been given you to throw away. You can't! You can't!"

He made a sharp gesture that checked her.

"My dear Maud, there are a good many things I can't do, and one of them is this. I can't hold any woman against her will—no, not if she were my wife ten times over. I wouldn't have let her go to Spentoli.

"But Bunny is a different matter, and if he wants to know all about her past, her parentage, he can come to me, and I can satisfy him. Tell him that! But if he really loves her, he won't care a damn—any more than I do."

"Ah!" Maud sighed.

She stood a moment, looking at him, and in her eyes was that mother-look of a love that understands. She held out her hand to him.

"Thank you for telling me, Charlie," she said. "Good-bye!"

He held her hand.

"What have I told you?" he asked abruptly.

She shook her head.

"Never mind now! You have just made me understand, that's all. I will give your message to Bunny—to them both. Good-bye!"

* * *

A chill wind blew across the ramparts, bringing with it the scent and the sound of the sea.

There was no moon in the sky tonight, only the clouds flying over the stars, obscuring and revealing them alternately, making their light weirdly vague and fitful.

Across the park an owl called persistently, its

eerie hoot curiously like the cry of a human voice through the rustling night. The trees were murmuring together down by the lake, as though some mysterious news were passing to and fro among them.

And, once more, alone on his Castle walls, Saltash paced restlessly up and down.

It was his last night at Burchester, so he told himself, for many a year to come. The fever for change was upon him. He had played his last card and lost. It was characteristic of the man to turn his back upon his losses and be gone.

His soul had begun to yearn for the wide spaces, and it was in answer to the yearning that he had come up to this eagle's eyrie. He could not be still, and the feeling of walls around him was somehow unbearable. But he expected no vision tonight. He walked in darkness.

The sound of the turret-door banging behind him recalled him to his surroundings. He awoke to the fact that the wind was chill and that a drift of rain was coming in from the sea.

With an impatient shrug he turned. Why was he lingering here like a drunken reveller at a table of spilt wine? He would go down to his yacht and find Larpent—Larpent who had also loved and lost.

They would go out on the turn of the tide, the two losers in the game of life, and leave the spilt wine behind them.

Impulsively he strode back along the ramparts. The game was over, and he would never play again; but at least he would face the issue like a man.

No one, not even Larpent, should ever see him flinch. So he reached the turret-door—and came abruptly to a halt.

It was no vision that showed her to him, standing there in her slender fairness, wrapped in a cloak that glimmered vaguely blue in the glimmering starlight.

Her face was very pale, and he saw her frightened eyes as she stood before him. Her hands were tightly clasped together and she spoke no word at all.

The door was shut behind her, and he saw that she was trembling from head to foot.

He stood motionless, within reach of her, but not touching her.

"Well?"

She made a curious gesture with her clasped hands, standing before him as she had stood on board his yacht on that night in the Mediterranean when she had come to him for refuge.

"I've come," she said in a voice that quivered uncontrollably, "to tell you something."

Saltash did not stir. His face was in shadow, but there was a suggestion of tension about his attitude that was not reassuring.

"Well?" he said again.

She wrung her hands together with a desperate effort to subdue her agitation and began again.

"I've come . . . to tell you something."

"Something I don't know?" he questioned cynically.

She nodded.

"Some . . . some . . . something you don't want to know. It . . . it was Maud made me come."

That moved him a little. That piteous stammer of hers had always touched his compassion.

"Don't fret yourself, *ma chère!*" he said. "I know all there is to know, all about Rozelle, all about Larpent, who I understand has been to see you and explain everything, and all about Spentoli."

"You ... you don't know this," said Toby. "You ... you don't know ... why I ran away from you ... in Paris!"

"Don't I?" he said, and she heard the irony of his voice. "I have an agile brain, my child. I can generally jump the gaps pretty successfully."

She shook her head with vehemence.

"And how do you know about Spentoli?" she demanded suddenly. "Who told you that?"

"The man himself," said Saltash.

"Ah! And what did he tell you?"

A note of fierceness sounded in her voice. She seemed to gather herself together like a cornered animal preparing to make a wild dash for freedom.

Saltash made her a queer, abrupt bow, and in so doing he blocked the way before her, so that she could only flee by the way she had come.

"He told me nothing that I did not know before, nothing that your own eyes had not told me long ago."

"What do you mean?" breathed Toby, pressing her clasped hands tightly to her breast.

Her eyes were still upraised to his; they glittered in the dimness.

Saltash answered her more gently than was his wont.

"I mean that I know the sort of inferno your life has been, a perpetual struggle against odds that were always overwhelming you. If it hadn't been so, you would never have come to me for shelter. Do you think I ever flattered myself that that was anything but a last resource, the final surrender to circumstance? If I had failed you . . ."

"Wait!" Toby broke in tensely. "You're right in some things. You're wrong there. It's true I was always running away . . . as soon as I was old enough to realize the rottenness of life. Spentoli tried to ruin me, but I dodged him, and then . . . when he trapped me . . . the hell-hound . . . I did my best . . . to murder him!"

The breath suddenly whistled through her teeth.

"I tried to stab him to the heart. God knows I tried! But . . . I suppose it wasn't in the right place, for I didn't get there. I left him for dead . . . I thought he was dead . . . till that day in Paris.

"And ever since . . . it's been just a nightmare fight for life . . . and safety. I'd have tried some other dodge if you hadn't found me. I was not quite down and out. But you . . . you made all the difference. I had to go to you."

"And why?" he asked.

She rushed on regardless of question. The flood-gates were open; she was hiding nothing from him now.

"You came. If you'd been an angel from heaven you couldn't have been more wonderful. You helped me . . . believed in me . . . gave me always . . . the benefit of the doubt . . . made a way of escape for me, made life possible . . . even . . . even . . . beautiful!"

She choked a little over the word.

"I offered you just everything. I couldn't

help it. You were the only man in the world to me. How could I help worshipping you? You . . . you . . . you were always so splendid . . . so . . . so great. You made me . . . you made me realize . . . that life was worth having. You made me . . . believe in God."

She broke into sudden wild tears.

"And you didn't love me enough even to take the little I had to give! I didn't want you to marry me. I never dreamt of such a thing. I had kept myself from harm, but I knew very well I wasn't fit to be your wife.

"Only . . . I loved you so. And when I knew that Bunny was turning against me . . . would never believe in me . . . I just couldn't help turning to you again. And then . . . and then . . . you went and married me!"

She wrung her hands tragically.

"I ought to not to have let you. God will never forgive me for it. I don't deserve to be forgiven. But I loved you . . . I loved you!"

She covered her face and sobbed.

Saltash reached out a hand and took her by the shoulder.

"Nonette! Nonette!" he said in a voice that was strangely uncertain. "Don't cry, child! Don't cry!"

She drew herself away from him.

"Don't . . . don't! I don't want you to. I just came to tell you, that's all, in case you should think I ever . . . cared for . . . Bunny. Maud says . . . you ought to know that. We only . . . only . . . played together. We never . . . really . . . loved each other.

"I wasn't his sort . . . or he mine. He doesn't

want me back. I wouldn't go if he did. I ran away . . . with that damn cur Spentoli . . . to give you a chance . . . to drop me. I couldn't face you after you knew everything. You'd never loved me, and I'd tricked you too badly. I knew you'd want to get free.

"Why didn't you start in and get a divorce? Why didn't you? Why didn't you?"

She suddenly lifted her face, storming the words, electrified, as it were, by the wild force of her passion. Again he reached a hand towards her, but she eluded him with a desperate gesture.

"No! No! Don't touch me! Don't touch me! I can't bear it! I'm going now! I'm going right away. You'll never see me again . . . never hear of me. And you'll be free! Do you understand?"

She paused a moment.

"You'll be quite free. I'll keep that promise I made to you. It won't be difficult. No one shall ever know how . . . and only you . . . you who never even pretended to love me . . . will be able to guess why."

She turned about with the words and wrenched furiously at the door behind her. In another moment she would have been gone. But in that moment Saltash moved, perhaps more swiftly than he had ever moved in his life before, and in a flash he had her in his arms.

She fought for her freedom then, like a terrified animal, twisting this way and that, straining with frenzied effort to escape.

And when, his hold encompassing her, he broke down her resistance, pressing her indomitably closer and closer till she lay powerless and

palpitating against his breast, she burst into ago-
nized tears, beseeching him, imploring him, to set
her free.

"Why should I?" he said, still holding her.
"Don't you know yet that it's the very last thing
I mean to do?"

"You must! Oh, you must!" she cried back.
"You can't ... you ... you can't ... hold me ...
against my will!"

"That's true," said Saltash as if struck by
something. "And are you capable of leaving me
against mine?"

His hold relaxed with the words, and instantly she sprang away from him, sprang like a fleeing
bird upon the low parapet beside them, and in a
second was sliding out upon the narrow ledge that
surrounded the great stone buttress of the turret.

"Hell!" ejaculated Saltash and gave a great
leap as if he would pursue her, then with abrupt
effort checked himself.

He stood with one foot on the parapet and
watched her, and in the vague starlight his eyes
burned with the old mocking, devilry behind
which he had so long sheltered his soul.

"So you think you'll get away from me that
way, do you?" he said and laughed his giving
laugh. "Well, you may try. Either stay there till
you've had enough, or throw yourself over! I'll get
you in any case."

She came to a stand, her hands spread out
on each side of her, her eyes turning back to him
across the awful space that yawned between.

Sheer depth was below her, but she did not
seem aware of it.

"I will throw myself over," she said with tense purpose, "unless you promise . . . unless you swear . . . to let me go!"

He laughed again, but there was no mirth in the glittering eyes that looked back at her, neither mirth nor dismay, only the most arrogant and absolute mastery that she had ever encountered.

"I promise nothing," he said, "except that one way or the other I'm going to have you. You can take your choice. You can sink or swim. But you won't get away. There is a bond between us that you can't break, however hard you try.

"Fling yourself over if you think it's worth it! And before you get to the bottom I shall be with you. I'll chase you through the gates of Hades. I've travelled alone far enough. For the future— we go together. That I swear to God!"

Across the abyss he flung his tremendous challenge, the laugh still on his lips and in his eyes the blazing derision that mocks at Fate.

And as she heard it the girl's heart suddenly failed her. She began to tremble. Yet, even so, she made a last desperate bid for pride and freedom.

She clutched at the cold stones on each side of her with nerveless, quivering fingers.

"There is . . . no bond between us! There never . . . never has been!"

He flung back the words like a missile, unerring, blindingly direct.

"No bond between us! Good God! Would I follow you through death if there were not?"

And then suddenly, with an amazing change to tenderness that leapt the void and enchained her where she stood:

"Toby, Toby, you little ass. Don't you know

I've loved you from the moment *The Night Moth* struck?"

There was no questioning the truth of those words. A great sob broke from Toby, and the tension went out of her attitude. She stood for a few seconds with her head raised, and on her face the unutterable rapture of one who sees a vision.

Then, with sharp anguish:

"I can't come back!" she cried like a frightened child. "I'm going to fall!"

Saltash straightened himself. His forehead was wet, but he did not pause for a moment.

"I'm coming to you. Keep as you are and I'll give you my hand to hold!"

She obeyed him as one dazed into submission. Blindly she waited, till with a monkeylike agility he also had traversed that giddy ledge to where she stood.

His fingers met and gripped her own.

"Now," he said, "come with me and you are safe! You can't fall. My love is holding you up."

She heard the laugh in his voice and her panic died. Mutely she yielded herself to him. By the strength of his will alone she left the abyss behind.

But when he lifted her from the parapet back to safety, she cried out as one whom fear catches by the throat, and fainted in his arms.

*   *   *

Out of a great darkness the light dawned again for Toby. She opened her eyes, gasping to find that the scene had changed. She was lying upon tiger-skins in Saltash's conical chamber and he, the king of all her dreams, was kneeling by her side.

That was the first thing that occurred to her, that he should kneel.

"Oh, don't! Oh, don't!" she said quickly. "I am not . . . not Maud."

He regarded her humorously, but the old derisive lines were wholly gone from his dark face. His eyes held something that was unfamiliar, something that made her quiver with a quick agitation that was not distress.

"So I am only allowed to kneel to Maud!" he said.

She tried to meet his look and, failing, hid her face.

"I . . . I know you have always loved her," she murmured rather incoherently. "You couldn't . . . you couldn't . . . pretend to . . . to . . . to really love anyone else . . . after Maud!"

There fell a brief silence, and she thought the beating of her heart would choke her. Then there came the touch of his hand upon her head, and its wild throbbing grew calmer.

"No," he said, and in his voice was a new, deep note unknown to her. "I am not pretending, Nonette."

The light touch drew her as it were magnetically. With a swift, impulsive movement she raised herself, gave herself to him, hiding her face still more deeply against his breast.

"But you . . . you . . . you couldn't really love me!" she whispered like an incredulous child. "You sure you do?"

His arms went round her, holding her fast. He made no other answer. Saltash, the glib of tongue, and ready of gibe, was for once speechless in the presence of that which has no words.

She nestled closer to him as a little furry animal that has found its home. Her incredulity was gone, but she kept her face hidden.

"But why didn't you tell me before?"

He bent his black head till his lips reached and rested against her hair.

"Nonette, you told me that I had made you believe in God."

"Yes?" she whispered back rather breathlessly. "Yes?"

"That's why," he said. "You got me clean through my armour there. Egad, it made me a believer too. If I'd failed you after that, well, He'd have been justified in damning me, body and soul!"

"But you couldn't!" she protested. "You couldn't fail me!"

His dark face twisted with the old wry grimace.

"I've failed a good many in my time, Nonette. But no one ever trusted me to that extent. You practically forced me to prove myself."

A little gasp of relief came from Toby. She spoke with more assurance.

"Oh, was that it? You were just trying ... to be good?"

"Just ... trying!" said Saltash.

"You still trying?" Toby asked, a curious little note of laughter in her voice.

"I shan't keep on much longer," he returned, "unless I get what I want."

"There'd be a blue moon if you did!" remarked Toby impudently.

Saltash raised his head abruptly.

"By Jupiter! There is one! Let's go to her!"

Toby's face shot upward in a moment.

"Where?"

Her eyes sought the skylight above them and the dim, mysterious blue of the night. His hands came down to her in a flash, dwelt upon her, caressed her, drew her.

She turned sharply and looked at him.

"Charles Rex!" she said reproachfully.

He took her pointed chin and laughed down at her. His eyes shone with a great tenderness, holding hers till they widened and shone back with a quick blue flame in answer.

"As I was saying," remarked Charles Rex royally, "when I was interrupted some six months ago, I have never yet refused a gift from the gods."

"But you've taken your time over accepting it, haven't you?" said Toby with a chuckle.

He bent to her.

"Let's go, my little one, my life, my only love!"

ABOUT THE EDITOR

BARBARA CARTLAND, the celebrated romantic author, historian, playwright, lecturer, political speaker and television personality has now written over 150 books. Miss Cartland has had a number of historical books published and several biographical ones, including that of her brother, Major Ronald Cartland, who was the first Member of Parliament to be killed in the War. This book had a Foreword by Sir Winston Churchill.

In private life, Barbara Cartland, who is a Dame of the Order of St. John of Jerusalem, has fought for better conditions and salaries for Midwives and nurses. As President of the Royal College of Midwives (Hertfordshire Branch), she has been invested with the first Badge of Office ever given in Great Britain, which was subscribed to by the Midwives themselves. She has also championed the cause for old people and founded the first Romany Gypsy Camp in the world.

Barbara Cartland is deeply interested in Vitamin Therapy and is President of the British National Association for Health.

Barbara Cartland's Library of Love

The World's Great Stories of Romance Specially Abridged by Barbara Cartland For Today's Readers.